You couldn't be arrested for flirting, could you...?

Sage slid her hand along Ian's forearm, catching her breath at the hardness of the muscle there. Ian was no desk jockey.

"My time is almost up. I'll be a responsible member of society again. There's nothing to say you and I can't have a more *personal* relationship, right?"

Ian's head snapped up at her touch and his eyes took on an intense expression. Sage pulled back in surprise—she'd never thought he was capable of such heat.

Wowsa. A little frisson of excitement danced along her hot skin at making him lose it. This was *fun*.

"You're completely out of line. There's nothing between us, and you know it."

"You sure about that?" Laughing, she headed to the doorway, making sure he got an eyeful of her short clingy dress.

He'd buried his heat under that cool unflappable exterior once more and she was intrigued. The sense of challenge that led her to computer hacking—the urge to unlock the forbidden—tugged at Sage now. What fantasies and feelings would she find inside this man?

She waved flirtatiously to Ian as she left. Some challenges were just too good to resist....

Blaze™

Dear Reader,

Thank you for reading the first book of my new HOTWIRES miniseries. In *Fascination,* rigid, stick-to-the-rules Ian Chandler confronts his forbidden desires concerning sexy computer hacker Sage Matthews—who also happens to be a convicted felon under his watch. If these two are going to make it together, they will have to not only cross the line, but meet in the middle, where the sparks are sure to fly.

Writing my first miniseries has been fraught with challenges and joys, and part of that was getting to create an entire cast of characters whose relationships grow over the course of three books. I've become very close to these characters as they have emerged on the page. I hope they will become memorable for you, as well.

Fascination is set in Norfolk, Virginia, at the mouth of the beautiful Chesapeake Bay, so I am donating a percentage of my earnings from this series to conservation projects on the Bay. Check for more details on this, as well as news on the upcoming HOTWIRES books, *Friction* (Jan 2006) and *Flirtation* (Feb 2006), as well as contests and news at my Web site, www.samanthahunter.com.

Warm wishes,

Samantha Hunter

Books by Samantha Hunter

HARLEQUIN BLAZE

FASCINATION
Samantha Hunter

HARLEQUIN®

TORONTO • NEW YORK • LONDON
AMSTERDAM • PARIS • SYDNEY • HAMBURG
STOCKHOLM • ATHENS • TOKYO • MILAN • MADRID
PRAGUE • WARSAW • BUDAPEST • AUCKLAND

For Mike, with love.

To my family and in-laws for all their constant support
and enthusiasm about my writing—you all make it fun,
and I appreciate you bragging about me!

And for my mom, Dorothy, who had her birthday at Christmas,
when this book is being released. I miss you, but I
hear you cheering me on every day.

RECYCLED PAPER
RECYCLED PAPER

ISBN 0-373-79228-X

FASCINATION

Copyright © 2005 by Samantha Hunter.

1

"SO DID YOU STAY OUT OF trouble this month, Sage?"

Sage Matthews held Ian Chandler's steady gray-eyed gaze for a long moment and pursed her lips, as if she had to think carefully before speaking. She looked down at the drink she held in her hand, slipped the straw between her cherry-red lips and sucked slowly, drawing her cheeks in so that her mouth formed a sexy pout around the plastic, closing her eyes as the cool burst of carbonation hit her throat. She released the straw and caught a stray bit of fizz with her tongue before answering.

"Exactly what kind of trouble would you be referring to, Ian?" Her soft southeastern Virginia accent added a lilt of mischief to her sultry purr.

Ian sighed, his full, gorgeous lips drawing into a tight, impatient line, and Sage felt a little spark of satisfaction. Ian might be the sexiest man she'd ever met, but she fought any attraction she'd ever felt because he was also a huge, unforgivable thorn in her side.

Sure, he was only doing his job, but for five years he'd controlled almost every aspect of her life. Annoying him—and teasing him—was one of the few ways she had to wrestle that control back into her hands. It was a small advantage, true, but she made the most of it.

It was an additional benefit that the air-conditioning in the Norfolk Police Department, where Ian had his new office—part of the new job he was leaving his post as a federal agent for—was on the fritz. The sweltering August heat created a fine film of sweat on her skin, making her thin tank dress cling to her, leaving little to the imagination. Sage didn't want to be subtle. She wanted federal agent Ian Chandler, who specialized in computer crime, to sweat.

She hadn't worn anything underneath the light shift because she was more comfortable that way but also because she was going to see Ian for her monthly check-in. *The more to tempt you with,* she thought devilishly. Sage didn't really want Ian, she just wanted to torture him with what he couldn't have. She slid a glance over his handsome features. She had a weakness for dark-haired men. Ian was a sexy guy. Too bad he was a cop.

But just five more days and she would be free of Ian for good. And hopefully free of a past that had been holding her back for too long. Her sentence for the computer crimes she'd been arrested for almost five years ago was nearly over. Ian Chandler was the federal agent who'd arrested her and he'd been assigned to "monitor her progress" throughout her sentence.

What that really meant was that he had the right to invade every corner of her life, watch her constantly, ask her anything he wanted and pry into every detail of her activities. If he caught her doing anything he thought broke the rules, he could throw her in jail. No questions asked.

It rankled her that he had so much power over her life, though she'd learned to live with it. Sage was determined never to give him the satisfaction of catching her slipping up—or *any* kind of satisfaction, for that matter. But he couldn't arrest her for flirting.

Not that he'd ever expressed interest. Ian was the epitome of straight and narrow. It wasn't in his nature to break the rules or back off from enforcing them. She tempted him incessantly, knowing he would never cross the line. But that fact only made pushing the limits all the more enjoyable.

She got up out of the chair and sat on the corner of his very organized desk. The room was clean as a whistle, the chrome gleaming, the windows sparkling clear. Everything was exactly in its place, and Sage pushed a neatly stacked pile of papers carelessly to the side as she made room for herself. She leaned over to throw her empty paper cup in the garbage can, not-so-subtly inviting him to take a peek at what was revealed by the slight sag of her neckline as she did so.

He just looked away.

She smiled and crossed one slender leg over the other, swinging it as if to some unheard song playing in her head, and picked up a pen to play with between her nimble, tanned fingers.

"Oh, you know I've been good, Ian. I'm *always* good."

Sexual innuendo aside, she *had* been good—not that she had much choice. As much as she liked to mess with Ian, she had no desire to end up in prison, so she'd also played it straight and narrow, as contrary as that was to her nature. There was no way she was going to lose what precious little freedom she had. She'd been a fool for a man once, which was what had gotten her into this mess in the first place. She wasn't about to do it again.

The first eighteen months of her sentence had been pure hell—house arrest, ensured by a nasty ankle bracelet that she could have removed herself within an hour if doing so wouldn't have landed her directly in a cement cage.

It seemed extreme for simply letting a virus out on the Net—especially when she had been duped into doing it. Not that anyone would believe her. Technically she *had* released it, but the fact that she had no idea what was on the disk she'd slipped into the computer that day didn't matter.

She'd told the one of the investigators who'd questioned her that she hadn't written the virus, but he'd clearly thought she was just trying to slip the rap. And she hadn't been able to prove otherwise; even to her own eyes the evidence was damning. Locke, the hacker who had set her up, had made sure of that.

The worst of it was that she'd been banned from any use of computers for five long years, a heavy price to pay, though it was better than prison. The judge had made use of flexible federal sentencing guidelines and had been cruelly creative.

If Sage was so much as seen near a computer, even in a store, or if she attempted to contact her hacker friends from college, she would go to prison. She wasn't allowed to own or use anything even remotely computerized, not even a cell phone. Ian was the man who'd tracked her down in the first place and he was in charge of making sure she minded her p's and q's. Sage had never been one much for p's and q's.

Ian's interference in her life had been considerable—she had to check in with him monthly; he'd stopped by her home unannounced, checked out her house and her habits, checked on her classes when she was in school and later would discuss her with her boss and coworkers at the plumbing store where she currently worked.

She had even caught him going through her mail on a couple of occasions. She'd never felt safe talking on the phone, though most of her conversations were innocuous—she didn't have many friends, as most of them had been computer junkies just like her. The loss of control over her own privacy was the worst punishment anyone could have concocted, sometimes overwhelming her.

No part of her life had been safe from Ian's prying. Once she'd been kissing a date good-night in front of her apartment and had found out later that Ian had run a background check on *him*. She'd discovered this at her monthly meeting when Ian had asked her not to see the guy again because he had a drunk-driving record. She'd railed against the unfairness of it, not that it could change anything.

Since then she'd stayed away from men, except for Ian. Eying him speculatively, she spoke again, "Ian, there's something I wanted to ask you."

"What's that?"

"Well, I am almost done with my time. I'll be a free and responsible member of society again within the week. And since you'll be starting a brand-new position and you won't be a federal agent anymore, you won't be held back by those silly ole rules that say you and I can't have a more *personal* relationship, right? So maybe we could—"

She reached over a little farther and slid her hand over his forearm, catching her breath at the hardness of the muscle there, and pursed her lips appreciatively— Ian was not just a desk jockey. The same crisp, black hair that he wore nearly military-short was sprinkled over his skin, and she wondered how it would feel to tangle her fingers in it over his chest and in other places....

Ian's head snapped up at her touch. His eyes weren't cold or distant now, but they were definitely pissed off. She bit her lip, partially because his reaction nearly sent her rocketing off the desk and back into her chair and partially because she'd never thought he was capable of such *heat*. Did it all just come from anger? Or was there more to it? Right now those irises were dark as slate, and she felt herself falling into them, forgetting the moment at hand, where she was, who he was.

Wowsa.

She'd never really seen him angry. Usually he was just aloof. A little frisson of excitement danced along her hot skin at making him lose it, if just a little. Now, this was *fun.* He yanked his arm from under her hand and pushed his chair back, distancing them.

"I don't have to tell you that kind of behavior is completely out of line. There's nothing between us and you know it. And there never will be. I think it's time for you to go."

She just laughed and got down from the desk, walking slowly around the office, posing in the doorway while turning to look at him, turning on full vixen mode.

"You sure about that?"

"Dead sure. I'll see you next week at your release hearing. Behave yourself until then."

He'd sucked that heat right back in and buried it under the cool, unflappable exterior once again. But now she was intrigued. All of a sudden the sense of challenge that had led her to computer hacking in the first place—the urge to find your way into somewhere forbidden, to solve an unsolvable puzzle—tugged at her.

What would it be like to try to get behind those straight-and-narrow walls that encased Ian so securely? What would be the key that would allow her access to what lay behind them? What would she find there, inside the man who always seemed so tightly under control?

She smiled, waving flirtatiously to Ian as she left the office. What the courts didn't realize is that you didn't get rid of a hacker by taking away their computer— hacking was a way of life, a philosophy, a way of thinking. And some challenges were just too good to resist.

"ANY LUCK YET?"

Ian looked up to see Marty Constantine standing in his doorway and shook his head noncommittally. "We'll see. Have the first interview today."

"When do you think the team will be up and running?"

Ian sat back in his chair, stretching and leveling a look at the man who was both his close friend and his immediate superior. He'd worked frequently with Marty over the years in his position with the FBI and Ian had nothing but respect for the man.

Though nothing had ever been said, Ian knew that Marty was the reason he had been offered this cherry opportunity so early in his career. It was fairly unusual to move from the federal government to local law enforcement.

Ian had spent the past ten years working on the FBI's Computer Crime Task Force. Fresh out of grad school at the green age of twenty-three, he'd worked his way up through the ranks. But even so, it would have been another few years before anything like this would have been handed to him at the federal level, if ever.

He'd lived his job. It had cost him friends. It had cost him his marriage. It was also the one thing in his life he was good at and it was his number one priority. His dedication had paid off, if not personally then professionally.

He'd jumped at the chance to create his own investigation team, even though it was a small team in a small department in a medium-size city. Norfolk, the site of the largest Navy base in the United States, had a huge government presence.

Local businesses and citizens were suffering increasing financial losses due to a spike in the number of computer crimes. These were situations street cops and even detectives weren't normally trained to handle, so computer-crime labs were being set up in cities all over the country these days, and Norfolk had finally found room in the budget to do likewise.

And thanks to Marty Constantine, Ian had been asked to get the project off the ground. Hopefully it would keep him in one place for a while. Working for the federal government had him chasing felons all over the map. Where trouble went, so went the FBI.

In his new position as team leader he might even see his own bed for more than a few nights a month. With any luck, maybe he'd find someone to share it once in a while. Women weren't exactly interested in someone who worked long hours, was gone at the drop of a hat and didn't know when he would be back.

"Hard to say. Could be within the month, or within the week."

"What's the problem?"

"Lots of applicants, but only a few stood out. I'm looking for a certain kind of person—expert, flexible, experienced. Since it's a small team, I need people with some chops."

"It's up to you, but this is a pretty high-profile project. Taxpayers' money and all that. Let's make sure it works."

"It'll work."

Marty nodded. "Things tied up at the agency yet? No pressure—we appreciate you coming in and getting started here a little sooner than scheduled."

"No problem, Mart. I have a few things left to finish. Shouldn't be a big deal."

"Like what?"

"You remember the LadyBug case?"

"Of course—it was one of the first big feathers in your cap, bringing her in. Sage Matthews. How's she doing? I still remember the pictures from the news. Man, she was a hot one, huh? Even looked good in handcuffs."

Ian sighed deeply, rolling his eyes. "She's at the end of her sentence. Her release hearing is next week, so I'm just finishing up on that. One more trip to court and I'll send her on her way, fill out some paperwork with the agency, then I'm all yours."

"Good. I'm looking forward to meeting the new team members when you have them lined up."

"I have someone coming in any minute now."

"Who is he?"

"She. Sarah T. Jessup. She's driving down from New York for the interview. We've used her from time to time as a freelance consultant."

"Otherwise meaning an informant?" Ian could detect the skepticism in Marty's voice—informants were not exactly the cream of the crop in police circles—but Sarah was operating on a different level.

"A good one. She's offered us first-rate information over the years with no expectation of compensation or recognition. She has managed to dig out things on the Net that we wouldn't have found, she can go places we can't. She's been…useful."

"Is she cute?"

Ian sent a disparaging look in Marty's direction. "This is a job interview for HotWires, Marty, not a dating service. Try to drag yourself up into the twenty-first century. Besides, I have no idea if she's cute or not—we've only communicated online and over the phone."

"Hey, I'm just thinking good thoughts for you, buddy. The national statistics say the median age for a second marriage is thirty-four. At thirty-three and counting, you are ripe for the plucking, the way I see it."

Marty grinned, clearly knowing he was pushing Ian's buttons and appearing to be thoroughly enjoying it. Ian stemmed his gut-level response, keeping his buttons in check.

"Statistics lie. I have no plans to rush into remarrying."

"Rush? Um, yeah, it's been a little more than five

years since the divorce, bud. You're a real wild man with the rushing. National stats say that most men re-marry within four years—"

"Marty—"

"I'm just *saying*. Maybe Sarah T. Jessup will be the one to make you a statistically viable member of soci-ety again."

Ian shook his head and took a long drink of water. He had no intention of gracing that comment with a re-sponse. Sarah Jessup could look like a *Sports Illus-trated* swimsuit model, but as far as Ian was concerned it made no difference—work and sex never mixed. All he cared about was how good she was at her job.

He *was* curious about her, though. Using the online name TigerLily, she had a reputation as a major com-puter junkie—a hacker in the most positive sense of the term. Not all hackers were criminals. In fact, the major proportion of people who called themselves hackers were upstanding citizens. Criminal hackers took other-wise creative and essential computer skills and used them recklessly to do harm or for their own gain.

Then there were hackers, like Sage and her friend Locke, who called themselves "hacktivists"—hackers who used destructive hacking methods as a form of so-cial protest, attacking the computer systems of multi-national corporations and major polluters and the like.

Unfortunately the attacks these groups waged often ended up hurting a wider spectrum of people than the organizations they targeted. Hacktivists were still often criminal hackers, as Ian saw it—you couldn't start letting politics be an excuse for committing crimes.

Sarah was an example of a legal hacker, someone who was just damned talented with a computer and who had no intention of breaking the law. She had become a self-appointed informant for the feds, tracking down Internet porn rings in her spare time, sending Ian what she found. It was a weird hobby, but the info she'd shared had led to several busts.

Ian knew that Sarah had an incomplete college degree and no formal police training, but those things could be dealt with. She had several part-time jobs, lived in a low-cost apartment in the city. He was willing to bet she probably spent more money on computer equipment than food. But she knew her stuff and stayed on the right side of the law, and that's what he was looking for. He trusted his gut about people more than he trusted pieces of paper anyway. He just had a feeling about her.

Taking a deep breath, Ian furrowed his brow in irritation as he detected the slightly spicy fragrance Sage had worn earlier today still lingering in the otherwise musty air of his office. His hand clenched tightly around the plastic bottle as he felt the familiar wave of desire hit, followed by the dulling sense of frustration.

Sage was a criminal hacker, someone off-limits to him even if only for the next few days. She was the last connection to his old life, and when this gig was over he would cut her loose and forget about her.

Yeah, right. Even though he'd carefully guarded against it, Sage had become more than just another case. He replayed the moment her hand moved over the skin of his arm and felt a flash of heat—he could still feel it, her soft skin on his. Her long fingers touching him just for that short moment. Her nails, ragged and bitten to the quick, were painted with red polish, and he found that was amazingly sexy, because it was on *her.* That she would wear such a bold color on her short nails was also indicative of Sage—she just didn't accept limitations. Not easily anyway. And she tempted him every chance she got.

He was tempted, no doubt about that. What red-blooded man could have Sage in front of him for years, issuing invitations left and right, and not at least *think* about it? But red-blooded as he might be, Ian's sense of self-discipline was fierce.

It also helped that he knew the come-ons and flirting were just her way of punishing him, of exacting some small bit of revenge for how he'd invaded her life. She didn't really want him, she just wanted to get back at him. He was just doing his job and he reminded himself of that every time he let himself think how good she smelled.

There was just something about her that he'd known from the start was going to be trouble. One look into those stubborn green eyes when they'd first met, and a part of him knew she could cause trouble for him as no other woman had. Her wildly curly red hair cinched it.

She was like a flame, dancing around him, always just out of reach.

He just had to hold strong. And he had.

Five more days.

It was his duty to keep tight tabs on her, and he had, but maybe he'd put in a little more time than usual. He told himself it was because she couldn't be trusted, because he couldn't drop the ball for one minute with her. He knew the type. They were like drug addicts with computers and were bound to cave sooner or later. But she never did, at least as far as he knew. Still, he watched. Carefully. And he would to the very end.

Marty took another bite from the apple in his hand, the crisp crack of the fruit snapping loudly in the quiet office, breaking the spell of Ian's thoughts. He cleared his throat. "Sorry. Lots on my mind. Anyway, Jessup's due in here in a few minutes, so I have to get ready."

Marty smiled and saluted. "Gotcha. Let me know how it goes."

Ian watched Marty leave and sighed as his friend nearly collided with a woman who appeared in the doorway—an incredibly tall, voluptuous, sable-haired Amazon with blue eyes that grabbed aggressively onto Ian's and didn't let go. Dressed in tight black jeans and a leather jacket—not exactly job interview attire—she didn't disappoint his expectations. Sarah wasn't your typical computer geek—she looked like hell on wheels.

Ian raised an eyebrow as Marty shook his fingers in a "too hot" gesture behind Jessup's head as he moved past her into the hallway—something she shouldn't have seen but did. Turning slowly, she fixed an icy-blue stare on Marty until he smiled feebly and slinked away.

Ian liked her already.

2

Sage sat nervously in the small lounge, the folder containing her résumé—her very *thin* résumé—clasped in her hands. The appointment for her interview had been more than thirty minutes ago, but she was willing to wait—she needed a new job, a real job, something that would allow her to move forward in life.

When she'd seen the classified ad for a security consultant, her heart had leaped—plenty of hackers, even those who had been on the wrong side of the law, became high-level security consultants. It was like hiring a reformed thief to help you make sure your house was secure. She figured she stood as much of a chance at the job as anyone.

But as time passed, her confidence was evaporating. The other applicants looked younger than she was, were male and their folders appeared to be much thicker than hers. Most had laptops with them or at least Blackberrys or PDAs. Probably none of them had felony convictions.

Was she nuts? There was no way a reputable company like this was going to hire someone like her.

Swallowing the lump of anger and despair that had suddenly formed in her throat, she left the room with as much dignity as she could manage, passing by the other applicants, who barely spared her a glance. Well, goody for them, she thought belligerently. Boring bunch of yuppie wannabes anyhow.

Except she wanted to be one, too. Wanted to be normal, to have a real life. Wanted to be respected for her talents. Wanted to be valued and accepted. She wanted to show her family that she could be a success, even though she had let them down in so many other ways.

Walking out into the stifling summer air, she yanked off the conservative gray blazer she'd spent way too much money on for the interview. Her hopes had been too high when she'd received the phone call responding to her application—an application conspicuously missing any hint of her conviction. She'd figured it would be better to try to explain that in person. Ha. What had she been thinking? She was just glad to have left before she'd gone in there and humiliated herself.

Lifting her face up, the strong rays of the midday sun felt like a kiss on her skin. The sky was clear and bright, but when she looked forward and tried to see her future, it was just a gray blur, on the personal as well as the professional front.

Regardless of the games she played with Ian, there hadn't been many men in her life. Not many decent guys were turned on by a woman who had been convicted of a felony. Those who were weren't the kind of men she wanted to know. How much of that would change when she was free?

Standing in the middle of the sidewalk, she let the warmth soothe her until a pointed wolf whistle had her glaring at the source and continuing on her way. She walked down the sweltering city sidewalk to the waterfront, gazing out at the Elizabeth River—Lizzie, as the residents called it. She leaned over the rail that ran the length of the park and led down to the Nautilus naval museum, the gigantic battleship, the USS Wisconsin, looming above the museum building.

It was a perfect day—the waters were smooth and green, and dolphins were frolicking out in the river as they often did, drawing amazed stares and the clicking of tourist cameras. Turning from the rail, she headed toward the hot dog stand in search of some lunch and companionship.

She'd taken the day off from the shop to go to the interview, so there was nothing else on her schedule. She'd given her two weeks notice anyway—motivation for getting a better job—but now she thought maybe she had been a little hasty in that decision. Feeling down, she knew just how to lighten her spirits. As she approached the stand, she heard the gruff laugh she loved filling the air around her.

"Hey, Ray."

"Sage! My favorite girl. Woooo, look at you! All dressed up today!" The older black man leaned over and whispered conspiratorially, "Did we have a date and I forgot?"

Sage laughed, her mood brightening at the sound of his voice. She responded, her voice playful.

"No, you never ask me out. I'm still waiting. You're my guy, Ray, you know that." She planted a solid kiss on his rough cheek and Ray howled again. He handed her a hot dog with everything on it—just the way she liked it—and a cola.

She sat down on the cement-block wall behind the stand, munching while Ray served some customers. He'd been around as far back as she could remember. Her parents had taken her and her sister to lunch at the park every week when she was little. That's when she'd met Ray. He'd become a good friend and a sort of honorary uncle.

She'd continued to come by at least once a week until her arrest. The eighteen months at the beginning of her sentence, when she had been confined to home arrest, had been the hardest of her life for many reasons, but one of those was because she never got to visit Ray.

Helping himself to a hot dog, he sat next to her, took a bite, then spoke. "So what has you down here all dressed up, li'l girl? You should be working, huh?"

She nodded, swiping some mustard from her chin with her pinkie and sucking it from the end of her finger. "Yeah. I took the day off. Had a job interview."

"Hey! Good news! You're almost done. You have to come down here and celebrate on the day."

Sage smiled, but then it faded. "You bet. But *free* is a relative term, isn't it, Ray? I've reached the end of my sentence, but I feel like it will never really be over. I can't escape the past." She knew she sounded sorry for herself in spades, but she couldn't help it.

Surprisingly Ray laughed again, and she looked up, popping the last big of dog into her mouth. He shook his head.

"Well, you know, girl, I made my own mistakes an' been where you are. Been in worse. You have a college degree. I never had none of that, but it's no matter. We can do whatever we want. We make our own luck."

"Easier said than done."

"Depends on what you tryin' to do, don't it? You just gotta find the right thing, that's all." He cleared his throat and patted her arm. "Don't worry too much. I had a hard time, too, when I got out. People'll forget, it just takes a while. I kept at it, got enough odd jobs to get myself a cart and found myself a spot to sell lunch. Before you know it I had this stand, right here in this pretty park. No one else is allowed to have their stands here, the city said, just me. The mayor himself. Imagine that."

Sage smiled and nodded quietly, having heard the story a thousand times. She always enjoyed how Ray's face lit up with pride when he told it. But he'd only told her about his time in jail after she'd been arrested and become too ashamed to come around to see him. So he'd come to see her and told her he understood.

He'd never told her why he'd been sent up, but she just knew there was no way this gentle man had ever hurt anyone or anything. She never asked. He never judged, so she didn't either.

"I just want a normal life, Ray. A good job. You know, the regular stuff."

"Mebbe you aren't cut out for regular, missy. You're special. You just have to find your place. Just don't plan on coming down here and tryin' to edge old Ray out with your own stand." He laughed again, and she couldn't help but join in.

"No worries there, Ray. I wouldn't even try to compete with you. Everyone knows you're the best."

She threw her arms around him in a tight hug. Looking past his shoulder, she stiffened suddenly, her eyes widening as she saw a familiar figure coming into view.

Locke stood at the edge of the park, watching her. She hadn't seen him since before her arrest. She thought she might be seeing things and blinked, but he was still there. A cold feeling spread up from the base of her spine. Slipping out of Ray's hug, she studied Locke, her heart in her throat. What was he doing here? Why now?

IAN LIFTED A STEAMING cup of coffee to his lips as he reviewed Sarah Jessup's résumé and his interview notes from the previous day. He believed he might be looking at the first new member of his team.

True, her formal qualifications were a little light, but she could talk the talk and she was more than a little interested. There were lots of people out there with the right education, the right experience, but she had *passion*. There was a sharpness, an electricity about her that he liked. She knew computers inside and out and she was a born cop whether she knew it or not. He'd wondered why she never pursued a career in law enforcement and had to suppress a grin when she'd told him she'd thought about it but didn't like the uniforms. She'd been relieved to know the HotWires weren't required to wear them.

The lady had talent, but she also had secrets. He had seen the slightest flicker in her eyes when he'd mentioned doing a background check. When he'd asked her if there was anything she needed to tell him about, she'd closed up like a clam. He would have to see what that was about before hiring her, but he trusted his gut that she was one of the people he was looking for.

There was also no denying that she was, as Marty had made a fool out of himself noticing, pretty damned hot—a fact that left Ian cold. He couldn't drum up an even mildly sexual thought about Sarah Jessup, whose ample curves and chocolate-brown hair should have at least inspired one. This was doubly annoying because his mind kept wandering back to Sage's silky copper curls.

Ian couldn't seem to get Sage out of his head. He didn't like being distracted, and that fact urged him to either get the hell away from her or to take her up on what she was offering, to get her out of his system. He was dangerously close to the latter. What would she do if he did? How would she react? Was it all an act on her part or did she really desire him?

He slammed on the mental brakes. No sense going there. He'd gotten out of his office thinking a change of venue would freshen his mind and help him concentrate, but thoughts of Sage followed him wherever he went. It was well and good that it was almost over. Four more days.

He'd taken his laptop and set up at a table in a local waterfront coffee shop for the afternoon. It was a perk that he could avoid the office when he wanted to. He watched groups of tourists file out of the tour boats. A large cruise ship was moored in the background. Even from a distance the ship appeared enormous. His parents took several cruises each year, but he'd never been on one, preferring to spend his weeks off fishing with his brothers at their camp in Maine.

His mom and dad had both been career Navy until they'd retired the year before last. His dad had been a commander who had worked on submarines since he was seventeen; he'd spent the last twenty years as captain of his own boat. Ian's mom had been a nurse who'd eventually found her way onto the big ships, as well. And now they took their vacations on boats. Ian didn't understand it, but to each their own.

He sighed, realizing he wouldn't be taking another vacation for a while. He should contact his brothers—Jim, who was older, and Gabe, who was younger—and see if they could at least grab a weekend sometime soon before all of his time got sucked up by getting the new team up and running. Squinting out the window, his gaze gravitated toward someone too familiar.

Sage.

She was standing with the hot-dog-stand guy she visited every week. At this time of day, though, he would have expected her to be at work. He made a mental note to check out why she wasn't.

The old guy, Ray, had been convicted on charges of bank robbery back in the sixties, but from what Ian could tell when he'd read over the case, it had been a bad bust. Ray had been hung out to dry more or less because he was convenient—caught in the wrong place at the wrong time. There wouldn't have been much interest in finding justice for a poor black man back then. Sage seemed very fond of him.

Ian couldn't make out the look on her face, but he saw her hug Ray and then slowly move past him to stand on the edge of the walk, her attention focused across the street. She was staring at a man, not far from where Ian himself sat in the window. The guy looked roughly her age but slick and—Ian's gut signaled him—dangerous.

He was tall. Skinny but built—the kind of guy who always walked away because others underestimated him in a fight. His long hair was tied back and an earring shone in the sunlight. Ian couldn't make out exact facial features, but his hackles rose in response to the way the guy's focus was obviously pinned on Sage. They were making direct eye contact—silent communication streaming across the distance between them. They definitely knew each other.

Ian's internal radar sharpened. Something was up and it wasn't good. Though he'd never seen the guy before, he knew the look—he was a walking hacker cliché. Dressed in black, wearing a leather jacket on a hot summer day, he stood out like a sore thumb to anyone who knew the type. Apparently, like many criminal hackers, he had an ego bigger than his brain. Though they'd claim otherwise, they usually wanted to be noticed.

Ian waited to see what would happen, his body tense and poised in the chair. The man stepped back, taking an envelope from his jacket and sliding it into the large pot of flowers by the curb, nodding in Sage's direction before walking away.

A drop, Ian realized. And not even a very subtle one. This guy didn't really care if anyone saw him. Or maybe he was just arrogant enough to think no one was looking.

What was she involved in? Ian's blood first ran cold and then started to simmer—was she an idiot, getting involved with these people when she was so close to finishing out her time? Or had she been involved with them all along, playing Ian for a fool? Sage was clever, no doubt. Maybe more so than he'd assumed. Maybe for all his supervision, she'd found a back door. Maybe her constant flirting was not so much an attempt at control as a method of distraction. Was the guy part of her old group? She'd never given up any of their identities, though Ian knew she hadn't worked alone. Someone new? Were they lovers?

His jaw tightened as ugly thoughts raced through his mind. He held himself in check, resisted the urge to run out and confront her, to find out what was in the package. He intended to find out soon enough.

SAGE'S FINGERS WERE NUMB as she looked through the tangle of blood-red azaleas, her heart beating furiously, to see what Locke had left there. She glanced around carefully, trying not to be too obvious. She was taking a chance, but it wasn't an option to call for help or alert anyone—if Ian knew she'd even seen Locke, he'd throw her in jail without a second thought.

She didn't want to pick up the envelope, but neither did she want to leave it there. Biting her lip, she knew it was meant for her. If someone else found it, it could be just as damning; she had to know what was in there. She could just take it and destroy it so that nothing in it could hurt her or anyone else.

Locke had barely changed in five years, but seeing him made her realize how much *she* had. In an instant she knew she didn't want him back in her life and she feared for her freedom. He was tall and gaunt-looking in a very romantic, poetic way that had once appealed to her but now left her cold.

They'd met the summer before her junior year in college; he'd been an arts major, and she'd been in computer science. He'd been her first lover, and they'd had some good times. He was passionate and his adventurous spirit in bed had encouraged her own to blossom. Locke had been adventurous in other ways, too.

Though he'd studied art history, he was a hacker of brilliant proportions. He eschewed formal education and had taught himself everything he knew. And he knew a lot. He'd studied art as a form of camouflage. Who would suspect an art history major who studied restoration of renaissance paintings of being a master computer hacker? Sage felt the material of her jacket slide against the paper of the envelope and gulped.

Walking quickly up the street to her home, where she could inspect the package privately, she kept glancing around suspiciously, making sure she was alone. It wasn't good news that Locke had showed up now. Being seen anywhere around him could violate her sentencing agreement. It was a relief to reach her house.

Throwing her jacket on the hall table, she held the thickly padded envelope in her hands and just stood quietly for a few minutes. When she finally ripped at the paper, an old zip disk and a letter fell out. She bent to pick them up from the floor. The disk was unlabeled, and she certainly didn't have a computer to read it with. She opened the white slip of paper, feeling her heart sink.

To my LadyBug—

She closed her eyes when confronted with her old "nym"—her hacker pseudonym or nickname. Locke had christened her with it when he had discovered her budding talent for creating "bugs," computer viruses. It was something she had done for fun; she'd never let any of them loose on the Net. It was enough for her to try to make the code work. She'd broken into some sites—sure, most hackers did—but she'd never been destructive in any way. Everything changed when she met Locke.

Opening her eyes again, she read.

I know this must be a surprise—hopefully a happy one. I've never forgotten you. I can only hope you still care since you didn't tell them about me. You proved your loyalty. I've thought of you every day for the last five long years. I've missed you, baby girl.

Her skin crawled as she remembered how he'd always called her that and how she'd loved it, practically worshipping him, how he'd made her feel as if someone finally understood her. Locke had understood her—well enough to take advantage of her.

Remember the evenings we spent in the grotto planning our attacks? Well, it's done, baby girl. It's a true work of art, a testament to your sacrifice. I worked every day to finish what you started, and now it's finished and ready to go. When you're free, we'll celebrate this great accomplishment together.

Always yours, Locke

Sage's hands were shaking now, and the note fell from her hands to the floor. She stared at the disk, her heart in her throat. She didn't need a computer to know what was on it—it was the thing that would take away her freedom for good.

3

IAN WASN'T QUITE SURE what he was going to do; he decided to just play it by ear and see what developed. He'd let a couple hours pass so that she wouldn't get suspicious. But he'd been watching. She'd brought the package home, and he'd watched her through the window as she'd read something, seen her bend to retrieve an object she'd dropped on the floor. He wanted to know what it was.

His knock on the door received no response, but he knew she was in there and rapped his knuckles on the wood door again, harder. This time the door opened, his hand held up in midknock. Sage glared at him, seeming agitated but not surprised by his appearance.

"What do you want? It's late."

"Well, isn't that a charming way to answer the door."

"I don't need to be charming with you."

"True, and I don't need to explain a random visit. Open up."

Ian watched her move to the side and noted the tension in her stance and her expression. Something was definitely up. It wasn't completely unprecedented for her to display bad temper when he showed up unexpectedly, but this was different.

She was guarded, protective. He could see it in the way she wrapped her slim arms around her midsection and how her eyes met his with their usual belligerence but none of the sexy challenge he usually encountered.

She was scared. He wanted to know why and of what. Of him? Of being caught? Or of something else?

"Everything go well today?"

"Jesus, Ian, I just reported in yesterday. Is it the usual practice to harass your people when they get close to the end of their sentences?"

"You're making a pretty big deal over a random visit. And here I thought you were always glad to see me."

The uncharacteristic flirtation, laconic as it was, triggered confusion in those green eyes, and he watched her lower her head before perusing the room.

"You mind if I look around?"

"You mean I have a choice?"

"No."

Then something of the old Sage snapped into place, and she dropped her arms, placing one hand on her hip. "Yeah, I figured. Just try not to get too turned on by my bras hanging in the shower."

Sliding her a look, he moved forward, going through the motions as he picked up a pile of mail and glanced through it, then at her calendar. No appointments slotted in for today, nothing she should have missed work for.

"You didn't go into work today." Looking up, he saw her slight surprise. Good.

"I wanted a day off."

"Doctor's appointment?"

"What, you want to know the results of my Pap smear?"

"I just wondered why you took the day off. They said you'd given final notice, as well."

She leaned against the doorway, the white cotton T-shirt she was wearing pulling across her breasts as she stuck one hand in the pocket of her shorts. The little colorful clips that held some of her wild curls in place made her look impossibly young.

"Yeah. I did." Her chin tipped up in challenge. "I hate it there. I'm leaving after my sentence is over, so you have no say in the matter. I want out of that place and away from you as soon as possible. I'm looking for a new job."

"So that's what you were out doing? Job hunting?" Made sense, he thought, remembering her outfit. Though it could also just be a cover for whatever else she was up to.

He'd checked out all the visible surfaces—no envelope. She'd hidden it or destroyed it, which made him even more suspicious. He'd have to do an extensive search to find it, but he couldn't look around more than normal without raising her suspicions. He wanted to keep her off guard for the time being.

He continued his inspection, not really looking around so much as mentally scrambling to come up with a plan. He frowned. He had one idea, though it wasn't a good one. He crossed back to where she stood, waiting for an answer to his question.

"Yeah, actually I had an interview, if you must know."

"With whom?"

"Meyers and Dunn."

Ian furrowed his brow. He'd met Jim Meyers once or twice at social affairs. He didn't like him. The guy was a sleaze who didn't even bother to hide it, married but never showing up to occasions with his wife. And the flavor of the month was usually someone just barely legal.

"For what position?"

"Whatever they have available."

Ian didn't even want to think about what positions Jim Meyers might have available for a woman like Sage. He made a mental note to check up on her application and drop a warning Jim's way. Then he reconsidered—her job hunt was not important and was probably just a cover story anyway.

"Don't you think it's putting the cart ahead of the horse to quit before you have a job?"

"Please, Ian, I'm too old and you're too young to be acting like my father."

Sage pushed away from the wall, and awareness dawned on him immediately. She'd been guarding that entryway—that's where she didn't want him to go. He looked down at her, gauging his next move. She appeared more slight than she usually did, the way the worn cotton just hinted at the even softer shapes underneath distracting him for a moment.

He didn't particularly like what he was about to do, but it was the only thing he could think of. He modulated his voice a bit, stepping slightly closer. She smelled like heaven. It made his job easier—and much more difficult.

"Believe me, darlin', I don't feel any paternal inclinations toward you at all."

She met his eyes then, and he saw the curiosity fighting with the caution. Then he blinked, and she turned to her old tricks, definitely trying to challenge him. She'd seen her chance and she was going for it. Fine— two could play that game. And he'd been at it longer. He might only be seven years older than she was, but in terms of experience, that was a lifetime.

"Good, because I'm all grown up, Ian." She stretched her arms over her head, yawning, and he watched as her shirt lifted, exposing her stomach, pulling taut across her breasts. Did the woman ever wear the bras that were supposedly hanging in the bathroom? Not that he cared. The less she was covered up, the better.

Reaching forward, he caught her raised hands in the air, trapping both of her wrists in one of his large hands and holding them there. Startled, she tried to pull away, but he didn't let her.

His heart slammed against his chest, his breath coming a little short as he felt her hip nudge him intimately, her scent suffusing the air around him. But while his body was responding of its own accord, his mind was in total control. Ian was confident—he never lost control unless he wanted to.

He wanted to find out what was in that package and he couldn't think of a better way to gain entrance to that room. She'd been using her sexuality to distract him for a long time, to chip away at his control—what would she do if she thought she'd finally succeeded in making him lose it? If she were confident that she had finally gotten to him, would she drop her guard? He decided to find out.

And if he was honest with himself, he wanted to find out more than that. He wanted to know her taste, to know how she felt under his hands, to know if she was as sweet as he imagined. He'd been fantasizing about sinking his hands into those copper waves and he wanted to do it, to know if she was as silky as she looked. It was wrong, but as long as he stayed in control, he could ease some of the curiosity that plagued him, this once. It was a calculated risk, but he'd taken them before.

"What do you think you're doing?" Her voice was breathless, and while her eyes were still guarded her face became rosy, and her nipples budded against the T-shirt. So it wasn't all a charade—she was attracted to him. At least physically. That was enough.

Though she was obviously deceiving him about other things, she couldn't hide her desire for him. Basic male satisfaction with that fact settled deep inside of him, and he hardened, stepping even closer to let her feel his response. Her eyes deepened to a mossy jade, and he fought an unexpected spike of desire. He needed to stay in control of the game.

"Hey, you made the offer, sweetheart. I guess I had some time to think about it. We're only talking four days. I don't want to wait that long. But if you want me to leave, I will. I'm not into forcing women."

The shocked look on her face was erased as she smiled up at him, but the smile didn't reach her eyes.

"No, I don't imagine you would ever have to, would you?"

It was all he needed to hear. Backing her up against the door frame, he crashed his mouth into hers, not bothering with preambles or gentleness. All of the anger he'd felt mixed with the passion that had been building for so long, during all those years she had been beckoning him. Now he was answering that call.

If she'd resisted, he would have backed off, but she only momentarily tensed before opening hungrily to his search of her mouth. Then she began a search of her own. In the back of his mind he kept a part of himself distant, away from the desire that was quickly consuming him. She was sweet and hot, a seductive combination of girlish innocence and sheer wanton lust. He felt his head swim a little but held on.

How far was she willing to go with this? How far was he willing to let her go? He lowered her arms so that they wrapped around his neck, and she clung to him. He growled his satisfaction at her submission against her lips.

The game was on.

SAGE WASN'T SURE WHAT had just happened. It had been a long time since anyone had touched her like this—though as the moments passed she was increasingly sure that no one had *ever* touched her exactly like this, so expertly, so thoroughly.

Ian was everywhere—his hands, his mouth. He was devouring her and she was letting him. It was heaven. She'd never imagined, not really, exactly what he would taste like, feel like. The reality was stunning.

Coffee. Male. Sex.

She'd been desperate to keep him from looking through her small dining room, where she'd slid the envelope under the carpet just seconds before she'd met him at the door. If he found it, there would be no explaining.

She'd only meant to piss him off a little, get him off the scent and out the door. She certainly hadn't expected *this*. Had he followed her all day? Did he know about Locke? The questions had frozen her in terror when he'd appeared at the door.

But as his warm hands kneaded her breasts, she realized his random evening visit might have been a ruse, a reason to come here. To see her. To seduce her and take her up on her offer—an offer she had never really meant to be taken seriously. Her concern about the envelope—and her ability to think at all—dimmed as he continued his sensual onslaught.

Ian was apparently taking it *very* seriously. She moaned into his mouth and nipped his lip as he pulled sharply at her nipple, sensations from the tug shooting down to her sex, creating an almost painful ache. He chuckled huskily and pushed his thigh between hers, rubbing against her intimately in a way that had her gasping and quickly losing any remaining reason.

Then he pulled back, looking down at her with glittering steel-gray eyes. The look he gave her was hard but hot. She couldn't see anything, read anything, except desire—he wanted her. And determination—he meant to have her. She shivered in excitement.

"This inspection seems to be a little more thorough than the rest." She tried to tease, though her voice sounded foreign to her, hoarse with arousal.

He smiled slightly, and she felt herself dissolve. She'd never seen him smile. Not once in five years. Even though it wasn't a full-on, happy smile, it changed his whole face and transfixed her.

"I'm not quite finished. I'm sure there are some things you're hiding that I need to find. I'll have to look around a bit more."

Paranoia pricked at the back of her brain, though she chided herself. He was only playing, making a sexual entendre, responding to the banter she had begun. She met him eye to eye, daring him. No way would she back down now. She wanted him, which startled her, but she also wanted the challenge. Would he back off? Was he testing her? Could she finally make him break his own rules and go for it? For the sake of the need that was throbbing through her body, she hoped so.

"Maybe you need to keep looking then."

He pulled her against him, kissing her hungrily as

he walked them both back to the sofa, only lifting his head as he pushed her back and stood over her.

"Oh, I intend to, sweetheart. Remember, you have no say in the matter. I can do anything I want. Look anywhere I want."

Her heart pounded in response to his words. The control he had over her life that she'd hated since the first day she'd met him suddenly felt incredibly erotic. He'd told her before he'd touched her that he wouldn't force her to do anything she didn't want, but now she couldn't think of anything she didn't want him to do.

He knelt down, sliding a hand up her thigh. "In fact, I wonder what you might be hiding right…here."

His fingers skimmed just underneath the hem of her shorts, and the muscles of her leg quivered in response. She stayed very still, letting the sensations ride over her, never letting her gaze move from his. His eyes darkened again as his fingers moved farther up underneath the material, scraping lightly against her soft curls, and she inhaled sharply, as did he.

"No panties. I'll have to make a note about that on the report."

"Uh-huh." She couldn't think as he petted her and she tested herself, staying as still as could be.

"Don't you want to move against me, sweetheart?"

"Yes."

"But you won't?"

"No."

"I want you to."

"I know."

He chuckled again and leaned over her, pushing her shirt up with his other hand and closing his lips around her turgid nipple, sucking lightly as his fingers found their way between the damp folds of her sex, pressing intimately against her. She trembled, panting hard, but didn't move as her body was overtaken by the building pleasure his ministrations were causing.

Ian moved his mouth all over her, leaving wet kisses all over her breasts and stomach as his thumb massaged her clit. She cried out in need but remained still.

"I may need to take a closer look."

Her voice was thready, coming in pants as he pulled her shorts off in one hard tug.

"I…figured…as…much…."

As he settled between her legs and swiped his tongue over her delicate skin, pushed his fingers deeply inside of her, she couldn't hold out. He'd won and she didn't care.

Arching back, she bucked against him, letting the quick release pour through her like liquid fire, chanting his name.

Still shuddering, she sat up slightly, and he hooked one of her legs over the back of the sofa, spreading her widely as his mouth closed over her again, sucking and lapping at her until she dug her hands into his hair and pressed him more tightly against her. Crying out, she rocked into him as she came again, animal sounds bursting from her unbidden as she forgot everything but the suffusing pleasure that he gave her.

"Oh, God…Ian…" She lapsed back against the back

of the sofa again, spent, sweating and exhausted though he didn't join her but simply continued to kiss and stroke until she felt like melted butter.

Tiny residual orgasms flew from the ends of his fingertips through her body until she couldn't even think. Eventually he lifted up next to her and covered her mouth in a scorching kiss that tasted like her own sex. Then the kiss gentled and he eased back, looking at her.

Somewhere in the foggy recesses of her mind she realized he hadn't sought any satisfaction for himself and she smiled in anticipation of correcting that oversight. Once she had her energy back, she would show him two could play this game. Right now she was utterly slack. She wanted to say something, but she didn't even know what. Words were lost to her.

Ian sat on the floor, his hand absently stroking the damp hair that clung to her forehead, and she swallowed a sudden lump of emotion clogging her throat. She hadn't experienced a lot of tenderness from men in her life, and this little bit from Ian slayed her. She couldn't see his expression, but his touch was gentle. She let her eyelids drop but opened them again, for a second fighting the drowsiness that overcame her. Then she just gave in.

IAN SAT IN THE CHAIR across from where Sage still slept soundly, watching her. He'd made a big mistake, but he couldn't bring himself to regret it. Of the women he'd known, he'd never tasted passion as he had with Sage.

Even though he'd kept himself tightly controlled, her responses had nearly pushed him over the edge.

All he really regretted was that it could never happen again. He would never know what it would be like to lose himself in her body and he half wished he had taken her completely the night before. But it was too late for that now.

He watched her shift on the sofa. She looked so innocent, her face peaceful in sleep, her head a mass of tangled curls that were just as silky as he had imagined. She'd be awake soon—he could tell she was making the slow rise to consciousness.

Guilt pricked at him. His plan had worked. She'd fallen deeply asleep, freeing him to search her place thoroughly, and he'd found what he sought. The envelope lay in his lap. He'd read the letter from the man named Locke, the man he'd seen the day before. Obviously an old lover. Obviously trouble.

She looked too young, too chaste in sleep to be the cause of so much chaos in his life. But he knew she was far from innocent. He studied her, knowing she was still half naked under the sheet he'd tucked around her. The scents and flavors of her skin, of her sex, from the night before swamped him, and he clenched his fist on the edge of the chair. He'd do his job. He'd take her in. And then he'd move on.

Her lithe body bowed in a stretching yawn and then her eyes popped open. She was momentarily confused, and he watched as she remembered. Her eyes closed again, a smile forming. He felt a jab in his gut—was she smiling at the memory of what he'd done to her or at how she thought she'd fooled him?

Her head twisted, and she saw him sitting there. At first there was warmth in her eyes, but the second her gaze landed on the envelope on the table next to him, she snapped from sleepiness to panicked wakefulness.

Bolting straight up on the sofa, her face burned when she realized she was still nude from the waist down, and she clutched the sheet around her. The sight of her bare skin made Ian's pulse jump, but just for a moment. He schooled his voice to be cool and casual.

"Good morning. Sleep well?"

She lunged for the envelope. He snatched it first and faced her fury calmly.

"You bastard!" He raised an eyebrow as she stormed, several creative curses spewing from her well-kissed lips.

"Oh, tut, tut, sweetheart. Not much of a morning-after person, are you?"

"How *dare* you?"

He felt his hackles rise at her indignant tone, but remained cool.

"How dare I what?"

As she paced, tears filled her eyes.

"How dare you do…what you did! Just to trick me so you could search my place! You're slime. You're worse than slime."

Ian just chuckled. "Oh, c'mon, sweetheart. Like you weren't doing the same thing with the same intentions? It was pretty obvious you were willing to do just about anything to keep me from searching that room. I wanted to see exactly how far you'd take it."

"I'm going to report you."

He just shook his head. "There's nothing to report. I didn't coerce you, I didn't force you, I didn't threaten you. What happened happened because you wanted it to." He saw her face flame with humiliation and softened his tone slightly. "And because I wanted it to, as well."

She shook her head, obviously distraught, and sank to the couch. He steeled himself against any emotional reaction and tried to remember who he was dealing with. For all the wounded innocence, she was playing him as much as he was playing her. And probably had been for a while.

"I want to know what's going on. Then you're getting dressed and we're heading down to the station."

"I didn't do anything wrong. I don't want to go to prison."

"Not up to me. We'll have to see what the judge says."

"Ian, you have to believe me. You know I've done well. I don't deserve this. He just left it for me, I didn't know…." She stood up and closed the distance between them, her expression desperate. He felt a small sliver of doubt and ignored it.

"I saw the whole thing. I saw the drop. I saw you get the package. You're obviously involved in something. Something you shouldn't be. I'm just amazed you couldn't wait a few more days, but I guess the thrill of pulling it off right under my nose must have been too tempting, huh?"

She stared at him in shock. "You were there the whole time?"

He nodded. "It was a coincidence but a lucky one." He smiled harshly. "Though not for you and your friend, I guess."

The next thing he felt was her hand slamming into his face and he shook his head in amazement—it didn't quite knock him back but almost. Damn if she didn't have a good right hook, and now she was planning to use it again. He stopped her fist midswing this time and threw her arm back at her side.

"Should I add assaulting an officer?" He didn't even think she heard him, she was that furious.

"You rotten son of a bitch! You had it all planned! You planned to come here, to use me and then to arrest me! You're disgusting! No matter what I've ever done, it's nothing compared to what you did last night!"

She was crying, nearly hysterical with anger, and he grabbed her, pinning his arms tightly around hers, holding her next to him to avoid being hit as much as anything else. He squeezed her more tightly as she struggled, and finally she calmed but wouldn't meet his eyes. He spoke, his breath moving next to her ear, which unaccountably he had to steel himself against tasting.

"No. I didn't plan it. I never planned on touching you, ever, though God knows you've tempted me long enough. Last night just…happened. Though I'll admit I used the opportunity to search your house and I'm glad I did. But I didn't come here with the intention of seducing you."

She looked at him then, still indignant, and he felt anger push the words out of him. "Though from the looks of that letter, sweetheart, you're hardly one to be calling me out on the moral carpet. You're involved with this guy, but it didn't stop you from letting me have you last night, did it? Though maybe Locke doesn't care as long as you're doing your part for *the cause,* huh?"

He expected her to explode, but instead she went slack. Her head dropped forward, and he rolled his eyes, shaking her lightly.

"Cut the melodrama, darlin'."

She looked up, white as a sheet, her eyes almost black, and he experienced genuine concern. He'd gone too far.

"Okay, listen, I'm sorry for that last crack. I shouldn't have made this personal."

Nothing. No response.

"Can you stand if I let you go?"

She nodded vaguely, and he had no sooner loosened his arms around her than she pulled back and punched him in the gut. When he doubled over, she lunged for the package again, but he blocked her and grabbed her wrist in the process. She fought tooth and nail.

"Stop it now or I'll cuff you. I mean it. I'll take you down physically if you make me."

She froze at that and turned on him, her eyes blazing.

"No one—*no one*—treats me like that."

Ian felt a little stirring of admiration and quelled it. "Fair enough. So you'll tell me about this?" He tapped the envelope.

"Yes. But I don't know much."

He arched his eyebrow doubtfully and stepped back more carefully this time, making sure she wasn't coming in for another surprise attack.

"I don't want to cuff you, but you're under arrest, and we have to go down to the station."

She nodded.

"You have to get dressed."

"May I shower?" Her voice was distant, mechanical.

"I don't think so. Just get your clothes on and let's go."

She walked over to where her shorts lay on the rug and stood for a moment, bending to get them.

"Turn around."

"Sorry. No can do."

She laughed then and it pierced him. It was a sad sound.

"Guess you won't see anything you haven't seen up close and personal, hmm?"

Quietly he watched her dress and kept his eyes raised as much as he could. When she was more or less put together, he grabbed the envelope and followed her to the door.

Some days his job sucked.

4

SAGE SWALLOWED AS IAN pulled into the parking space in front of the station. She only had one play left and she was willing to do just about anything not to be taken into that building.

She rubbed her icy hands on her shorts, trying to warm them. It was hard to act sexy and calm when you felt like vomiting. She was desperate and didn't like the idea of what she was about to do, but the idea of going inside that building was making her physically sick. Anything would be better.

Ian opened the door and waited for her to get out. When she did, she did so slowly, swinging her legs out first, then raising herself up to stand just a bit too close to him. She anchored her lower lip between her teeth and looked up at him.

"Ian, I want you to listen to me just for one minute."

She stepped closer and planted the palm of her hand on his chest. His heart rate increased—she could feel it through the thin material of his shirt. She smiled up into his face, hoping her eyes were seductive instead of mirroring the desperation she was feeling inside. He looked around uncomfortably and pushed her hand away, removing it but not releasing it from his tight grip. His strong hands were warm and felt too good, though his voice was cutting.

"Don't even try, sweetheart. Don't lower yourself." But he wasn't immune to her closeness or the contact—she could tell. She saw it in his eyes. There was still a chance.

She stepped closer, keeping her voice just above a whisper so that only he could hear. Meeting his gaze head-on, she displayed a confidence she was far from feeling.

"Aren't you more worried about lowering yourself than you are about me? You still want me, don't you? Last night…last night, you only had a taste. A taste of what could happen between us. I'm willing to do more. To do anything you want. Just don't take me in there— please."

He blinked, considering her—or her proposition— for a moment. "I don't think so. Let's go." He started to step away, but she didn't budge. It was time to get down to it.

"Okay, fine. Let's put it this way. I don't know what's on that disk, but if anyone can find out, it's me. He gave it to me. Believe me, Locke won't make it easy. By the time you have one of your flunkies figure it out, it'll be too late."

"Too late for what?"

"To stop it."

His clipped tone was impatient and he stepped

toward her, menacing but closer, and she felt a surge of hope.

"Stop *what?*"

"I don't know exactly. My guess is some kind of virus."

"Your specialty, huh, *LadyBug?*"

She let the comment bounce off. "Yes. And you won't be able to figure it out without me. If you take me in there, you can forget it. I won't help you. I know him. I'll be able to find things you won't even know to look for."

He snorted. Looking away in disbelief, he started to pull her after him again, but she tugged him back, hard, pulling out of his grip, feeling panic crawl along her skin. But she didn't show it—she had to make him listen.

"I'm serious, Ian. You won't be able to figure it out in time. I can. Locke knows me. I—" She swallowed deeply, giving him some of the truth. "I can hand you Locke. I'll do it—but not if you bring me in there." Her eyes turned to the tall brick building and then returned to his.

"Whatever's on that thing, it's in your possession, and you know what they say about possession. You'll probably go to prison this time around."

"I don't care." She kept her gaze locked to his and played her final card. "I may go to jail, and your new position will go up in smoke when they know you had a chance to stop what was going to happen and you didn't." She gulped in a breath, not caring if he knew

how anxious she felt. "And they may not believe you
seduced me and maybe they won't even care, but it
might put a nice dent in your spotless reputation if a
rumor gets out. And I can make it sound far, far worse
than it was."

She saw something change in his eyes, if only for a
second, and knew she had him—she'd found the key.
His job, his reputation. The only things he cared about.
She pressed the advantage while she had it. Her tone
became pleading and eager.

"We can get him, Ian. Please. There are only three
days left to my sentence. Do you really think I would
get involved in something this stupid now? I'm not
with him—"

"You're his lover."

She nodded slowly. "*Was.* Years ago. Not now. Not
ever again would I be that stupid." He was teetering on
the edge, and she drove her point home. "Don't take me
in there, Ian, and I'll stop this, whatever it is he's doing.
Give me a chance."

He grunted in disgust and walked away, turning his
back on her. Relief started to ease its way through her;
he'd gone for it.

"How long have you been in contact with him?"

"I haven't been, I swear. Yesterday was the first time
I'd seen him in years." Disbelief flooded his features
and she stepped closer. "I'm telling the truth. I haven't
had any contact with Locke at all—I was shocked to see
him yesterday and I know I shouldn't have picked up
that envelope…."

"Shoulda, coulda, woulda, sweetheart. Why *did* you pick it up then? You know the rules." His eyes searched hers, and she opened her gaze to his—she needed to show him she wasn't hiding anything at this point, as much as he would believe that.

"I don't know." She stumbled a bit, the words tumbling out before she could stop them. "I was shocked to see him. I just acted on reflex. I didn't know what he left there, but I didn't want to take a chance."

"A chance on what?"

"That whatever was in there could harm innocent people. And believe me, it probably can."

"How magnanimous of you."

She swept past his hurtful tone and pressed on.

"I know it was stupid, all right?"

"No. You had options. You could have come to me, told me, or brought the thing to me first instead of hiding it."

She barked out a laugh, watching him blink in surprise. "What? And you would have believed me and not thought I was in cahoots with him anyhow? Like I could come to you on anything like that. There wasn't anyone I could go to."

"And I am supposed to believe you haven't seen him, your old lover, at all, in years?"

Her face was close to his as she lowered her voice to a whisper. "Couldn't you tell last night, Ian? How hungry I was, how I reacted as soon as you touched me? Couldn't you feel that I haven't been with anyone? Not for a long while."

He lowered his eyes from hers, his hands planted on his hips, and she wondered if she hadn't pushed too far. But when he looked at her again there was a flicker of temptation in his gaze.

"If you're yanking me here, sweetheart, I'll take you down."

"I know. I'm not. And the offer stands, Ian. I'll help you get Locke and I'll do…anything else you want."

IAN FIGURED HE WAS LOSING his mind, letting her get to him, letting her swing the game. But what if she was telling the truth? What if she was right? Bringing down this guy would be a much higher priority than busting Sage on a sentence violation, even though the rules said differently.

He looked into Sage's face, trying hard to be ruthlessly honest with himself—was he making a good judgment call, taking the lesser of two evils, or was he giving in to his baser instincts? She wasn't just offering him Locke, she was offering him herself. That was a dynamite package. One that could easily blow up in his face.

As much as he didn't want to admit it, he'd had doubts about bringing her in since they'd left the house. Even after finding the envelope he'd wanted to kiss her again as much as anything. *In for a penny, in for a pound,* a voice in his head mocked him. Was what he'd done last night any less damning because he hadn't been inside her?

But he had already made up his mind, for better or

worse. He looked closely at her. "How do you know I won't just turn you in anyway when this is all said and done? I could use you to find Locke, sleep with you and bring you back here. You could go to jail anyway."

He reached out and touched her chin, though it wasn't a tender gesture as much as a taunting one as he tipped her face up toward his. Her eyes remained steady on his.

"You're not that kind of man."

"You have no idea what kind of man I am. How much do you really know about me? Nothing. But I know everything about you, don't I?" His voice sounded harsh even to his own ears.

She smiled a little at that, not willing to let him grab the reins. "I guess I'll find out. I'm willing to take my chances. Anything is better than going in there."

"Even giving me your body, knowing there's nothing in the future for us? Not knowing if I'll keep my end of the bargain?"

She nodded, pinning him with a frank and open stare. "I've already given you my body. What I wonder is if you'll give me yours. I want you, Ian. It's simple as that. And I don't want to go to jail. Maybe I'm the one using you."

He was testing her, putting their situation in the coarsest terms he could, but she'd answered him without so much as a flinch. She was either being very honest or she was just very, very good.

He didn't touch her anymore, didn't stand closer—they were in a public place where people would recog-

nize him, so he couldn't risk it—but he was burning
with the desire to haul her next to him and show her
what she was doing to his sense of control.

He'd like to think he could hold out, that he would
never touch her again. That he would just work with her
to find Locke, then let her go. But her scent was still
on his hands from the night before, seducing him. He
knew he would take what she wanted to give him. He'd
have to deal with the consequences of that later on.

"Get in the car."

With those four words he sealed both of their fates.

APPEARING TO BIRD-WATCH, Locke sat on the park
bench, staring up at the trees through tiny binoculars.
He didn't like what he was seeing.

LadyBug was standing outside of the police station
with the fed, and he was holding the envelope in his
hand. Had his baby girl ratted him out? Gone to the
other side? Was she doing the cop? He spat in disgust
as he focused the lenses on her face. He knew that look.
He'd missed seeing it. Pure sex. If those two weren't
doing each other yet, they would be soon.

Anger faded as he contemplated the idea, and a smile
curled his lips. Maybe that was how she was working
him. The weakness she'd found to exploit. LadyBug
was a hacker to her bones, not as technically skilled as
he was, for sure, but she was inventive. She had good
instincts and she could figure out how to get into any
system—maybe she'd gotten into the cop's via his dick.

In which case, he supposed he could forgive her, but he'd have to watch some more to know for sure. He'd hoped she would wait for him. He'd wanted to have the pleasure of sinking in between her sweet thighs for the first time in five years. But if she had to make that kind of sacrifice for the cause, he could understand.

On the other hand, if she'd really turned, well…then he'd have to come up with a more severe punishment.

SAGE STARED OUT THE WINDOW as they turned the corner into the historic neighborhoods of Ghent and pulled to the curb. This was a place she knew well from her childhood. Her parents had several friends who lived in the wealthy section of the city, and she'd often played in these immaculately groomed yards, though she hadn't kept in contact with any of the friends she'd had here.

Ghent was the city's first "planned community," created at the turn of the twentieth century, far different from the cookie-cutter housing developments that littered costal areas nowadays. The place had real Southern charm. A variety of gorgeous Dutch Colonial- and Greek Revival-style homes nestled comfortably next to each other. The area was very peaceful and serene even though it butted against some very busy main streets.

When they'd hit high school, all of her friends had become involved in pep squads and cheerleading, yearbook club and sports, but she just hadn't been interested in those things. They all seemed so…light.

So she'd spent more and more time hacking, more

time sitting alone at the computer, honing her skills. The separation between her and any of the people she knew, including her own family, had widened. They certainly hadn't been able or willing to understand her lack of interest in cultivating a proper social life, particularly one befitting a teenage Southern belle.

Sage snorted to herself—she never had been and never would be a *belle*. Life might do its worst—send her to jail, deny her a decent job, whatever—as long as she was saved from being a *Southern belle*.

"What are we doing now?"

"We're going to see what's on this disk."

"Ian, I haven't eaten, showered or even brushed my teeth. I feel gross." Sage thought wistfully of the Starbucks down at the corner, exhausted and feeling the lack of caffeine in her system now that she had won the battle over being arrested.

"EJ will have something to eat. The rest can wait."

He got out of the car and headed toward one of the oldest, grandest homes Sage had ever seen in the area. This one had been kept in pristine shape. The austere look of the porch columns was softened by pink magnolia trees that blossomed in the yard. Dense ivy crept along the lower parts of the columns. Blooming flowers sat in pots in the corners of the porch, surrounding them in fragrance.

"Who's EJ?"

Her question was answered seconds after Ian rang the bell. The man who answered the door smiled widely at Ian, obviously happy to see him, and then politely acknowledged Sage's presence with a nod and a soft-spoken hello. As the two men exchanged words, Sage noted that EJ was a local—his accent was typical to the area, not the old-timer's thick accent that sounded like a foreign language, but the upper-class cadence that spun even casual speech into silk.

Even though Sage had the female version of the same accent, she could still appreciate how it made men's voices incredibly sexy and refined. It was a sign of someone born and bred—very well bred. EJ Beaumont—she caught his last name from the mailbox—was a real Southern gentleman.

The name sounded somewhat familiar, but she couldn't place it—perhaps he'd done business with her father. He was at least third-generation Virginian, she guessed. Idly she wondered what EJ's initial stood for—most likely his father's name and his grandfather's, as well. The initials probably allowed him to be referred to without confusion, a common convention.

EJ's friendly green eyes—almost the exact same color as hers—shifted from Ian to Sage. He was freshly shaven, crisp and cool regardless of the heat in khakis and a white cotton shirt. He was barefoot, his sandy brown hair neatly cut. He wore a musky aftershave that was pleasant and not overpowering.

Sage ran a hand self-consciously through her messy hair—she must look like a street rat in comparison, though he didn't give one glimmer of noticing, behavior befitting of a real gentleman. EJ smiled and shook Ian's hand, stepping back to invite them in.

"EJ, I was hoping you might have time to help me out with something. Something…delicate."

EJ's brow creased and he nodded. "Of course. I've just fixed a late breakfast—are you two hungry? There's plenty. I got a little carried away at the market this morning."

"Sounds good." Ian locked glances with his friend. "Are you alone?"

"Millie's upstairs getting dressed. She'll be down in a few minutes, but she'll be delighted to see you."

Ian slanted a skeptical smile, and Sage wondered who Millie was but didn't ask. Ian guided her ahead of him, his hand impersonal at the small of her back. Sage knew it was a gesture meant to move her where he could keep her in sight, not affection of any kind, but still his touch warmed her skin.

They followed EJ into the kitchen, not saying a word. She wondered what Ian was going to tell EJ about her. She walked to a beautiful cherry dining table, admiring EJ's taste, and he motioned for her to sit.

"Let me get some food and we can talk."

Ian sat directly across from her, looking tired and stressed. His blue chambray shirt was rumpled, his gray eyes a little bleary. The sensuous mouth that had brought her such pleasure last night was set into a firm line. He didn't make eye contact with her but glanced around the kitchen instead, making small talk as EJ carried some trays from the granite counter to the table.

The two men sat at the corner of the table, and Sage sat directly across, observing. Ian appeared rough-hewn set against EJ's more refined, gentlemanly manner. Ian's stone-colored eyes were cold next to the warm ocean-green ones of his friend, but just looking at Ian made her heart race.

The way his black hair fell over his forehead begged her to push it back with her fingers. She knew what he felt like, what he tasted like, and she knew being with him would be heaven with just a little bit of hell mixed in for spice. The memory was still sharp and made her intimate muscles clench slightly as she observed the angles of his face, more distinct with exhaustion, but she remembered how they'd softened when he'd made love to her.

Sage smiled to herself. Soft-spoken, refined gentlemen never had been her preference, much to her mother's dismay. EJ reminded her of her father a little bit—they had the same aura of the well-bred. Ian was more of a mystery, more of a challenge.

She sighed, thinking of her family more in the last ten minutes than she had in the last week. They'd moved from Norfolk two years ago, wanting to be close to her sister, who had just had twins in Charleston. Sage hadn't seen them in a while; she wasn't allowed out of the state.

She missed them sometimes but didn't know why. Just the sense of something familiar, something she belonged to even though she didn't exactly fit their mold. Of course, she'd never really tried.

She hadn't dated many boys and she'd gone out of her way to find ones her parents would be shocked by.

That was part of how she had ended up with Locke, no doubt. But her attraction to Ian was something new. Her parents might even approve of him, though he wasn't a native Southerner. It was something she would think about later. Right now she was starving.

"Oh, we have company! Ian! It's been forever!" A sweet, lilting voice cut through Sage's reverie. A petite, blond and gorgeous young woman entered the kitchen and went straight over to Ian, giving him a friendly hug before moving to EJ's side. The woman moved gracefully between the men, fresh as a daisy, dressed in a white summer sheath and sandals. This must be Millie. As Millie slipped her arm possessively through EJ's, Sage spotted the brilliant-cut diamond on her left hand as it sparkled brightly in the sunlight that lit the kitchen. EJ was clearly spoken for. Millie looked curiously at Sage, then back at Ian as he spoke.

"It's good to see you, Millie. You're as beautiful as ever," he said, gracing Millie with a charming smile.

Millie pinkened slightly, and Sage fought the urge to roll her eyes. So this was what Ian was like when he let his guard down for a moment. Sage was speechless. Everything about him had…warmed.

"And who is our guest? Is this a friend of yours, Ian?"

Sage ignored the tightening of her chest as she watched his face change, and as he started to speak, she interrupted. She didn't know how Ian would introduce her, but she didn't feel like being publicly humiliated in front of people like EJ and Millie. She stood, pushing her hand out across the table and taking Millie's milky white, French-manicured fingers in her own. She remembered how to do the lady handshake, though she despised it. It was so…weak.

"Hi, I'm Sage Matthews. I work with Ian."

The lie came out smoothly, but for some reason a small crease formed on Millie's smooth, pale brow. Then it cleared almost instantly.

"So this is a work visit? Well, any friend of Ian's is certainly welcome anytime."

She looked at the food EJ was setting on the table. "Darling, I see you've outdone yourself once again." Millie fluttered becomingly and smiled at Sage. "I'm so lucky to have found a man who loves to cook, but whatever the reason, I'm glad you're both here to help us eat all of this food. I swear, I will be a cow after a year of eating like this."

Sage highly doubted it, especially as she saw how carefully Millie made her selection from the food assembled before them. EJ accepted her compliment silently, smiling warmly at his fiancée and pulling out her chair, then sitting himself and gesturing to Ian and Sage.

"Dig in."

Sage didn't need to be asked twice and loaded a plate up with pastry, fruit and scrambled eggs, eagerly accepting the large cup of coffee EJ handed her. Ian filled his plate, as well, and the rest of breakfast was taken up with small talk about EJ and Millie's wedding plans. Sage only half listened, concentrating on one of the best breakfasts she'd ever eaten.

Ian kept the conversation centered on the couple and didn't bring Sage into it. He obviously didn't want to discuss their business with Millie present, which she was thankful for, no matter the reason. As the small talk faded, they ate quietly and a light tension stretched over the table.

Millie looked at Sage and then Ian. "I know you have business to discuss. I suppose I should make myself scarce."

Millie was apparently not pleased that Ian was bringing business concerns to EJ's attention. Sage wondered why.

Ian sighed, standing as Millie stood. "Mil, I do have some things to talk about with EJ, but it's been so nice to see you again. Don't let us chase you away from your breakfast."

Again he turned on the charm, and Sage wanted to gag. Well, not really, but still. Millie smiled and waved her hands at him. Was this the kind of woman Ian liked? The kind of woman he imagined marrying? Sage shifted uncomfortably in her chair, feeling even more grungy than she had when they'd arrived.

"No problem, Ian. I just worry that Ethan works too hard sometimes. But I'm his fiancée, not his mother. I have a lot to do myself and have lingered far longer than I should have. It has been wonderful seeing you again. And it's good meeting you, Sage. I'll leave you all to your business."

It was a polite speech, stiffly delivered. Her disapproval was obvious as she leaned in to kiss EJ on his smoothly shaved cheek, but no one said a word as she exited the kitchen. EJ looked at Ian in half apology.

"Sorry about that. She gets upset when she even thinks I might be having anything to do with law enforcement again. But it happens from time to time, even now, and she has to accept that."

"I know. I'm sorry we had to interrupt your morning, but this really couldn't wait."

EJ nodded, pushing his plate back. "Tell me."

Ian explained the events of the last twelve hours to EJ, who listened attentively, nodding and giving Sage the occasional glance.

She realized suddenly, while she listened to Ian explain, that he'd used her name sparingly, only in introducing her to EJ. In fact, he'd not used her name once since he'd shown up at her home.

What was going on in that head of his that using her name had suddenly became taboo? Whatever it was, she didn't like it. She realized as she pushed her empty plate away that EJ had addressed her. She looked at him, blinking and shaking her head.

"I'm sorry, I was lost in thought."

EJ just smiled, and she looked into his handsome face, wondering why she had never been attracted to men like him.

"I was wondering if you had any clue as to what might be on that disk?"

She shook her head. "It's an old zip disk, obviously. Knowing Locke, though, I wouldn't try to open it on a machine you don't want to self-destruct."

"A virus then. That was your specialty?"

She nodded and glanced Ian's way. "A long time ago. It's been a while."

"I looked over some of your files when you were arrested—Ian dropped them by for me, as I sometimes help him out a little with these kinds of things, you understand. There was some nice work there."

Sage couldn't help but grin when Ian's eyes looked as though they would pop right out of his head at EJ's statement.

"Thanks. But that code wasn't mine—most of it, in fact, was Locke's. I never set my bugs loose, I just liked to create them. I was only the delivery girl for that one."

EJ looked at her, clearly astonished. "You did time for a virus you didn't even create?"

Sage nodded, shrugging, looking squarely at Ian. "I figured who would believe that even if I told them? It didn't matter, I set it loose and my fingerprints were all over it."

"Locke set you up then?"

Sage nodded, and Ian leaned in a little, his voice low.

"I hate to break into this happy little hacker circle, but EJ, while I know as a programmer you might have some technical admiration for the programs Sage created, they were very destructive."

EJ nodded, his eyes just a little amused as they met Ian's intense gaze. "Sorry, Ian. It's just rare you come across that kind of finesse in programming."

Grimacing, Ian sat back. "And you expect me to believe, after all this time, that you were just set up? That this guy Locke was really responsible for that virus?"

Sage shook her head, no self-pity in her voice. "No, I didn't expect anyone to believe that, which is why I never said anything. What would have been the point? Locke had seen my code, he knew my style and he's a much better programmer than I am, so there was no way for me to prove it wasn't mine. But it's the truth."

EJ stepped in before Ian spoke again. "A lot of hackers create viruses just for the fun of it, Ian—it's not so far-fetched. You can get virus-writing programs right off the Internet, it's not a secret. I've written many in my spare time. The code Sage had was very…mature. I was surprised to find it came from the mind of a twenty-year-old, but now it makes a little more sense."

Ian interrupted him, still focused on Sage. "You expect me to believe you were completely innocent in all of this?"

"No." Her voice was quiet. "I wasn't innocent—I was stupid to get involved with him and I knew there was a virus on that disk. I just didn't know how bad it would be. Sending it out was like an initiation in the group, proof I would carry through. At the time I liked the idea of being a hacktivist, of making a difference in the world. In a way I still do, though I obviously don't agree with their methods anymore. But Locke said it was just going to mess up some Web pages in corporate offices—"

"Webjacking?" EJ asked and Sage nodded, continuing.

"It wasn't supposed to do more than bug up office computers with some politically targeted messages—generally harmless stuff in the scheme of things. At least, that's what he told me. It's one of the many reasons I would not be involved with him right now. He lied, he used me and he's the reason I was arrested."

"He doesn't seem to think you minded, according to your note. Does he really think you were so devoted to his cause that you would be willing to take that kind of fall and then he can just catch up with you years later, as if nothing has happened?"

She shrugged and remained silent.

Ian stared at her for another long minute, not saying anything before he dropped back in his chair. The silence at the table remained stultifying for a long moment. When he spoke, he didn't address her but EJ.

"So you can take a look at this for me?"

Sage frowned. He obviously didn't trust her to check out the disk and tell him what was on it.

"Sure. I have some victim machines upstairs."

Ian stood, obviously ready to get to work, and Sage admitted she was impressed. EJ must do some serious programming to have victims—computers that you could use to test programs that might crash them—lying around the house. In her teenage years she'd tested her programs on her own machine and had learned a lot by crashing it, then putting it back together again. She shifted in her chair, uncertain of what her role in all this was.

"Let's get at it then." EJ turned to Sage. "You want

to help? I imagine you might recognize what's on there faster than I will."

Sage stuttered, unsure of how to answer. Technically she was still under her sentence—she wasn't supposed to touch a computer. She looked at Ian, waiting for his call. He nodded.

"She can watch what comes up. But I want you at the keyboard."

EJ murmured a quiet assent, and they filed out of the kitchen. Sage trailed along last, feeling unsure and yet eager to know what was on the disk. It was obvious Ian thought she might still be in cahoots with Locke—he wasn't going to let her anywhere near the computer. Ironically whatever it was that they found, she just hoped it was serious enough to keep her out of jail.

5

IAN PACED THE ROOM, making phone calls and trying to dig up information on Locke while EJ and Sage huddled together in front of the computer. He didn't want to go through official channels just yet, considering his own indiscretions of late, so he called Sarah. She was good at digging and this might be a nice test run for her.

"Sarah? This is Ian Chandler."

"Oh. Yes?" Cool as a cucumber, as usual.

"How are you?"

There was silence for a moment on the other side of the line—Sarah wasn't much for formalities and never hit him as chatty. She was probably up to her eyeballs in some computer search. Predictably her reply was vague and distracted. He liked that she didn't just drop everything and kiss up to him just because he'd interviewed her for a job.

"Uh, fine. You?"

"Good. I'm working on a project that I thought you might be able to help out on. Consider it kind of a trial run for the team. I can get to see you work in the field."

"What do you need?" Her attention was razor-sharp

now; he heard it in her voice. To the point, no run-around. He respected that.

"I'm trying to dig up information on a hacker named Locke—"

"Locke? Really?"

Ian cocked an eyebrow at her impressed tone of voice and her interruption. "You know him?"

"I know of him, yes. He's into heavy stuff. He's about corporate sabotage, big money, that kind of thing. I've only seen some of his code, but it's wildly advanced. Way over my head."

"Do you know where he is now, what he's up to?"

She sighed into the phone. "He stays to himself. He's only seen when he wants to be. I've heard some people chatting about some new code on some message boards, so he's still in the game. I heard a rumor he was being approached by the corporations themselves to attack competitors. Kind of a computer special-forces guy. He's the real thing. Elite."

There was almost a sense of awe in her voice, and Ian cleared his throat. Hackers were a weird bunch.

"That's good to know. We have a line that he may be up to something big right now, but I could use some underground info. There isn't much about him—next to nothing—in the files. I'd like to know what he's been up to for the last five years."

"I'll do what I can, but I'm not sure how much I'll be able to find."

"Why do you say that?"

"He's slick, the original invisible man. I don't know

anyone who even knows him personally. I've never even heard or seen his real name. He doesn't hang out in the regular circles. Never gets caught. Usually uses his groupies to do his dirty work. They get busted, he gets lost. And they remain stupidly loyal to him. I think he could be a pretty ruthless guy, if the chatter about him is anywhere near true."

Ian blinked, looking at Sage, his mind absorbing what Sarah said.

"Ian?"

He returned his attention to the phone. "Yes. Okay—can you send anything you find to me by tomorrow?"

"You got it."

Ian murmured thanks and hung up. It was effortless working with Sarah. He trusted her already and knew she would deliver. He also liked that she was all business. No flirting, no complications. The bit about a trial run was a stall—he wanted her for the team, but he had to do the background check before he could make it official. The results on that would be in within a couple of days; he was doing an exhaustive check. She'd need security clearance to access government databases, and he wanted to know the people he was working with inside and out.

Sage's laugh rang suddenly, and Ian's attention snapped back to the room. Had he ever heard her really laugh? Sure, she had used that sexy chuckle on him, a sarcastic snicker, but he'd never heard the amazingly clear, lighthearted laughter she was sharing now—though not with him. Watching her lean closer in front of EJ, she pointed to something on the screen, and Ian felt a clutch of something nasty in his chest.

He walked over and stood behind them. "What's happening?"

Sage sat back in her seat, the laughter stopping. EJ nodded and kept staring at the screen, hitting keys as he spoke.

"Yeah, I think we have it mostly figured out." He spared a glance in Ian's direction. "Sage recognized it immediately—it's her code—but we've done a little extra digging."

"And you found something funny?"

Sage looked up at him sharply. "No, not funny at all. I wasn't laughing about that, it was—"

"It's not important." He directed his questions to EJ. "How could this be her code? I thought it was from Locke."

Ian didn't respond as the hot color that infused Sage's cheeks told him she wasn't happy about being cut off, but he trained his eyes on the screen, calming the intense agitation that had overcome him when he'd watched Sage sitting there laughing with EJ as if they were old friends.

Line after line of code swam before him on the monitor. He could make some sense of it, but programming wasn't his strong suit.

"So what does it mean? Is this our virus?"

EJ seemed a little struck by Ian's harshness, as well, and looked up, narrowing his eyes at his friend. "Since it's her code, Sage can fill you in."

"So what does it mean?"

"I have a name, you know. It wouldn't kill you to use it and to be even slightly aware that I am a human being, not some dog you can just kick when you feel like it." She rose, whirling on him.

Ian took in the high color in her cheeks, the furious breathing that caused her breasts to swell against the thin material of her shirt. He felt a small curl of admiration. He liked that she would stand up for herself, and it made him want her even more. Though he wasn't about to give much ground, he gave some.

"Sage. Tell me about your code."

"Figure it out yourself, you jerk." She spun, still angry, ready to leave the room, and he crossed to her in a second, grabbing her arm none too gently.

"And just where do you think you're going?"

She blinked but didn't waver. "Away from you."

"We have a deal, Sage." He said her name with more inflection this time, filling it with intention that was clear, and he saw the understanding in her eyes. "You help me, I don't arrest you."

Because of EJ's presence, he left out the other terms of their "deal," but he knew she understood when he dragged his thumb along the sensitive inner skin of her arm and saw her catch a breath. Pulling her arm away, she rubbed the spot, though he knew he hadn't been holding her hard enough to hurt her. He would never do that, no matter how much she pissed him off. And there was more in her eyes than anger now.

"Okay. Fine. Jeez."

Ian turned back to find EJ watching them speculatively before he discreetly turned back to the monitor and cleared his throat.

"Ian, this is an old piece of code, something Sage wrote long ago. Though it has some new notations in it."

"Notations?"

"Programmers keep notes in their source code—it reminds them of problems, keeps their place. Some of Sage's old programming notes are here, but there are new ones, things Locke wrote—to her, ostensibly, anyway."

Ian fixed his gaze on Sage again, directing his questions toward her. "What kind of notes?"

"He fixed bugs, closed a back door I had built in—he thought that was funny. He kind of graded it, like a teacher would, showing me all my mistakes."

"Why would he do that?"

"For fun. To show me how much better he is at this than I am, to assert his superiority. He always was kind of like a teacher."

Ian didn't say anything, but a tight feeling took over his chest again as he blocked ideas of what Locke must have taught Sage—and not about computer code. Even though it was years ago, the knowledge chafed him.

"So what is it?"

"It's an old bot."

"A bot is a small program that carries out some specific kind of function it's told to do," EJ explained.

"Yeah, it's distributed out on the Net and it finds a computer to hide away in and waits for instructions."

"What did your bot do, Sage?"

She smirked. "Nothing. I couldn't get it to work. But in theory it could do most anything you would want it to do—crash a computer, gather information—"

"What information?"

She shrugged. "Whatever you want. Credit card numbers, accounts, names and addresses, whatever payload you wanted."

"But the bot is only part of the program, right?"

She nodded. "Yeah, you have the worm or the virus that delivers it and then the payload—what it is supposed to get, or do."

"So why would Locke have sent you this now?"

Sage took a deep breath, meeting his eyes. "I'm not sure, but I guess it's a clue. He said he'd finished the program, and he can't just mean the bot. But he and I used to talk…." She drifted off, looking away, and Ian honed in, wondering what made her so uncomfortable all of a sudden.

"Talk about what?"

"I had this idea. You know, just a crazy idea, mostly. Most viruses attack computers—they mess up the networks, but they hit fast and hard, like the distributed denial-of-service attacks that hobbled major online companies in 2000. That makes them easy to detect and deal with within a few days. They do damage, cost money, but they are more or less controllable."

"And? What was your idea?"

"I just thought that wasn't enough. We were supposed to be trying to disable the companies we were objecting to—those who abuse third-world workers, who pollute the environment and deceive their workforces and their customers."

"Your 'cause.'"

She nodded. "But I couldn't see how individual attacks were doing all that much damage. A lot of hacking is social—you know, engineering relationships so they will work for you, allow you to get access or information. That's the basis of the markets, as well—people have to trust the seller to keep the markets going."

EJ had turned, paying close attention to Sage as she spoke. She was caught up in explaining now, her eyes bright with excitement.

"So I thought instead of these massive attacks that were debilitating but only temporarily, how could we really disable these corporations? We had to do it by disrupting the relationship they have with the consumer."

"So you needed to infect the consumer as well as the company," EJ said.

Sage sat back in her seat. "Yes, but not just their computers, their minds—affect how they think about online commerce. So I came up with this idea that you could send out millions of these bots. They would collect information as people made online purchases and send it back to a central database. Until they were supposed to do something, they would just sit quietly, unnoticed. They work very slowly, very stealthily, to avoid detection."

"Then what? What do they do?" Ian couldn't help being drawn in, as well, though he tried to maintain an objective attitude. Her story was like a good murder mystery.

"At a certain point a program would be executed that would start employing the information gathered by bots and infecting the transactions people made were making with online companies. For example, if they bought a pound of coffee, they would be charged for ten—things that seemed like normal errors, on individual accounts everywhere. Little at a time, though, and not all in one place."

"Bogging down the companies with fixing bad transactions," Ian chimed in.

"Right. But scale was the key—small bugs but so widely distributed that it made a real mess. It ends up discrediting the online commerce system, ruining the public trust in making online purchases. The program could be implemented over weeks, maybe even months, and eventually it would crash the trust people have in e-commerce. Vendors could fix it, but it's so small and slow, and companies would be in deep before they realized what was even there. People would be very hesitant to buy anything online anymore."

"Christ." EJ's exclamation was a whisper. Ian just stared at Sage.

"And you actually wrote this thing?"

She shook her head, balking a little now. "No, I

could barely write this little bot and get it to work. This was just brainstorming, you know, kicking around big ideas. But to actually be able to pull something like this off would take much more talent than I had. And a lot of time. It's a pretty enormous project."

"But maybe Locke did it? He finished it?"

She looked at him, her eyes serious. "Sounds like it. He had the time. You were asking what he'd been up to for the last five years, well…this could be it."

"Is there a way to find out what companies are targeted? Warn them?"

She shook her head. "You can guess it will be major retailers. I remember some of the ones we were after, but it's a crapshoot, depending on where consumers buy. You could hypothetically target it, I suppose, by tracking purchases and consumer records, but that would take a lot of time. Anyway, there's another problem. EJ found it."

"What's that?"

"The new bot is booby-trapped, for all practical purposes. There's a notation about a fail-safe in it that if Locke doesn't send the right command or gets shut down before it executes, it fatally crashes every computer it's planted in."

"Which could be millions?"

"Yes. Or more."

"So there's no way to stop it?"

"You'd have to get his computer—his mainframe—and shut it down from there before it executes. There's no way to tell where all the bots are and no real way to know all the companies he's hitting, at least not at first."

Ian walked over and stared out the window. Millions of computers crashed, paralyzing businesses, hospitals, governments, schools, personal computers—wherever these little programs had buried themselves—or a massive attack on e-commerce. Great choices. He turned back to Sage and EJ.

"I guess we have to find him then, and fast. According to the note he left with the disk, we can assume Tuesday's the day he plans to execute the program, in honor of your release. That gives us three days. Let's hope it's enough."

SAGE'S EYES WERE BLURRING. She and EJ had been sitting at the computer all day, digging deeper into the code, seeing what other hidden goodies they could find. Ian had been in the background, on the phone, though a few times when she had peeped out to see what he was doing, his charged glance had locked with hers as he'd continued speaking softly into the phone, not missing a beat.

Sage stretched in her chair. Watching someone else at the keyboard was so boring—she would much rather be driving than riding shotgun. But EJ was good—and he didn't seem to be faltering at all. The man had amazing stamina to sit and focus for so many hours, and she wondered idly what other kind of stamina he had, though she wasn't remotely interested in him that way. It had been, however, nice to sit with someone who smiled at her and who treated her nicely after putting up with Ian's gruff and distant manner for so long.

They'd worked right through lunch, and her stomach growled, loudly. EJ looked over, grinning.

"The beast is restless."

"You can say that again. Breakfast was great, but it's been a long time." She laughed, enjoying their camaraderie. He'd caught her up on a lot of things she'd missed over the years, explaining new programs, new viruses, new advents in the computer world. She was surprised to find out how much she'd missed. It had the dual effect of making her feel out of the game and making her itch to get back in it.

"So what do you want to do when you're free and clear? Just a few days now, right? It must be exciting."

Sage looked back at Ian quickly, then down to where her hands were clasped in her lap.

"I don't know. I thought I could find something in network security—you know, helping companies patch the weaknesses in their networks, that kind of thing. But you've made me see there's a lot I need to catch up on. Maybe I should take some classes. Maybe even teach someday."

"Taking some courses never hurts, but you know this stuff on an instinctive level. For the work you want to do, they're more interested in how attacks are done, how access is gained. In that sense, the basics never change."

Sage smiled, feeling encouraged, and launched into interrogation mode, getting as much information as she could. She was thrilled when EJ even offered to hook her up with someone in the field who might be able to help her get some consulting gigs to start with to help her build a name for herself. But the conversation—and her excitement—was quickly dampened by Ian's suddenly cool presence as he walked up, apparently catching drift of their conversation.

"What the hell are you doing?" He pierced EJ with a look that would make lesser men wither, but EJ just cocked an eyebrow.

"We're talking shop."

"She's not allowed to do that."

The eyebrow rose a little farther. "Don't you think it's a little late for that considering what we've been doing all day?"

"There's a difference between getting information off that disk and encouraging her to do it again."

"It's hardly that, Ian, and you know it."

Glowering, Ian looked down at Sage, and she ground her teeth, biting back a response. He was just being a jerk.

"EJ and I can talk about whatever we please. I'm going to find a good job and get out of that stinking plumbing-supply place where you stuck me—which, by the way, I never showed up for today so I am probably fired anyway and thank God for that. You have no say in what I do or what I talk about or to whom."

Her chin went up mutinously as his eyes glittered dangerously down at her, and she wondered if she had gotten a little too brave in EJ's presence and pushed a bit too far. Technically he did have a say, though it ran-kled her. Ian's gaze were back to EJ and he nodded curtly.

"Thanks for the help. We're going now."

"Why don't you stay for dinner and we can—"

As they spoke, the door opened, and Ian stepped back, avoiding it. Millie walked in, obviously surprised to see them there and not entirely pleased, though she was much too polite to say that. Ian recovered from the unexpected interruption first and smiled.

"Ian…how nice to see you…again."

"Just like a bad penny, huh, Mil?" Ian teased, trying to change the subject. "We were just leaving. Things took longer than we thought. Sorry to have interrupted you twice in a day."

Millie looked at EJ, questions in her eyes as she spoke. It was clear there was going to be a "discussion" between the two of them once they were alone. Sage felt a little sorry for EJ. Millie obviously didn't like her husband-to-be dabbling in law enforcement.

"I understand, of course. But I'm forgetting my man-ners. Are you staying for dinner?"

Ian just reached for the door handle. "Thanks, Mil, but another time—lots going on right now." He looked at EJ pointedly. "I'll be in touch."

EJ shifted a little uncomfortably, not quite meeting Millie's gaze. "I'll be around. You want me to keep at this?"

"You have time?"

EJ nodded. "I'll make it."

"I would love your help then. Thanks. You know where to contact me."

EJ nodded and walked them to the door. Sage bestowed a smile on him when he winked at her, his friendliness taking some of the sting out of Ian's blatant rudeness. She touched his arm briefly. "Thanks, EJ. Thanks for the tips on jobs, and I hope we can talk about that soon."

"I'll look forward to that."

They left, and Sage took a deep breath as she faced getting back in the car with Ian, who looked like a thunderbolt personified. It was going to be an interesting ride.

SAGE SPUN AROUND TO CLOSE the door to her house, glaring at Ian when he stood in the way.

"Do you mind?"

"Actually yes. You're slamming that thing on my foot."

She gave it another push for good measure, but he put his hand up, stopping it before it hit his boots.

"You need to pack. We'll get some dinner and then we have a long night ahead of us."

Staring at him dumbfounded, she blinked.

"What? Pack for what?"

"You aren't staying here—you aren't moving out of my sight until this thing is over. And I'm not staying here, so get what you need and we'll go to my place."

"I'd rather be here. This is my home." She felt exhausted from the long, tense day. She did want to be home. She wanted to shower and crawl into her bed and forget about everything. She turned away, walking from the door, not facing him. Too much had happened, and all of her ragged emotions bubbled too close to the surface. She needed some distance.

"Please, Ian. Just let me be for a while. I promise I won't take off anywhere."

Her heart sank when she heard the door click shut and then heard his soft footsteps cross the entryway to where she stood. When he spoke, his voice was softer, even a bit more gentle than usual.

"Listen, you can shower, get freshened up. I'll wait. But we only have so much time left and we need to use it all. I promise you'll be comfortable at my place. And you'll have your own room, if that's what's bothering you."

Sage could have dealt with him yelling, cursing or ordering her around. But the softness of his voice, something so rare and lovely, wrecked her.

"I—I'll just go shower then. Thanks."

She tried to make her escape, but his hand twirled her around, and she tilted her face away, but he took her chin in his fingers, made her face him. She couldn't cop an attitude if she tried—everything was there for him to see. His eyes had changed, too—they were softer, as well—and she just stared as he drank in every detail of her face.

She couldn't turn away from him. This new side of him, the side that urged her to lean in, to find comfort, stunned her. But it's what she did, and felt his arms close tightly around her as she heaved a sigh and soaked up the warmth of him. All of his gruffness and harsh words made these gentle moments surprising and sweet. She might have imagined his lips in her hair, but after a few minutes, he eased her away from him.

"Go. Get cleaned up. I'll be right out here."

She backed away, noting that he didn't look at her. Had the unexpected tenderness he'd shown her disturbed him as much as it had her? She headed for the shower, not sure what to think.

IAN UNLOCKED THE DOOR to his house, every bone in his body aching. Had it only been a day since he'd discovered the envelope at Sage's? In that time his entire world seemed to have changed.

He'd always been clear, always sure of decisions he made, and now he wasn't. He'd let a known felon talk him into not arresting her, he'd let her violate her sentencing agreement to help him get information and he'd made love to her. And worse, he wanted to do it again.

Sage *was* helping him, though. She'd been used by Locke—everything she had been accused of doing might have been false, at least to some degree. He wasn't sure what to do with that knowledge.

On the long drive to his home, the scent of Sage's skin and hair, made more fragrant from her shower and the humidity that hung heavy in the dusky air, had nearly driven him mad. He'd wanted to pull the car into the first available spot and devour her. Now she was stepping in his front door, looking around, taking in the view of the Chesapeake that graced the patio doors of his living room.

"Wow. Nice place."

"Thanks. I'll show you to your room and we can get some dinner."

She turned, looking refreshed in her red sheath and sandals.

"You go get showered and freshened up. Show me where things are and I'll cook."

He must have just stared blankly in shock because she waved her hand in front of him.

"Ian? Hallooo. Point me to the food."

"Your room…"

"That'll keep."

He nodded, feeling too zoned to do much more than agree. Adrenaline and lack of sleep were taking their toll. Showing her to the kitchen, he turned back. "Help yourself to whatever you want. I think there's some fish in there, if it's still good."

He left, oddly comforted by the sound of her moving around in the kitchen and yet feeling unsettled over leaving her there alone. What if she took off? Or tried to contact Locke? He shook his head. She wouldn't be that stupid—not so close to the end of her sentence. She'd already had one close call.

But to be safe, he stopped by the entryway and looked into her bag, snagging her keys and taking them with him. The only landline in the house was in his bedroom, and he patted his pocket for his own keys. He tried to relax and let it go, forgetting everything for a while as he stepped under the steaming water of the shower.

When he emerged, feeling more refreshed, he inhaled deeply—something smelled damned good. And he relaxed. If he was smelling food, she must still be here. Truth be told, he had hurried through his shower, just in case.

He pulled on a pair of shorts and a T-shirt, walking back downstairs in his bare feet, following the delectable scent.

Stopping in the doorway, he felt like one of those cartoon characters that the very large rock falls on. He watched Sage moving around his kitchen like a pro, humming softly and doing a little dance as she put a salad together. He saw the tuna fillets being kept warm on the grill and cleared his throat, letting her know that he was there.

Surprised, she turned, smiling at him, and he reeled—did a second rock usually fall on those cartoon characters? Because when she smiled at him like that, that's how he felt. Flattened. If she wasn't the most stunning woman he'd ever seen, he'd eat his shirt. Which he was almost hungry enough to do anyway.

His body seemed to be experiencing an odd little buzz, which could be due to hunger, but he thought it was more likely caused by Sage. He couldn't seem to take his eyes off her, and his body—certain regions in particular—was definitely responding. Suddenly he doubted the wisdom of having her here. He walked into the kitchen, enjoying the feel of the cool tile on his feet.

"Smells great. Is that lime?"

She nodded. "Made a lime-and-dill butter for the fish. Perks it up a little. I hope you don't mind it rare—tuna really is best that way."

Ian just blinked in amazement as he inhaled the heavenly scents again.

"I didn't know you could cook."

She smiled and her voice was almost teasing. "Hey, big surprise, there's one thing you don't know about me." Picking up the tuna and transferring it to a plate, she inhaled the pungent aroma and smiled. "I cooked a lot during my eighteen-month in-house—I needed to do something creative or I would have gone nuts. I'm surprised I didn't gain about fifty pounds."

"You must have a great metabolism."

"Nah, with so much time on my hands, when I was bored with cooking I just worked out."

"It must have been pretty hard. You don't seem like the type to do well cooped up."

She nodded and shrugged and didn't say anymore.

Ian cleared his throat and spoke cheerfully. "I'll get some wine. Want to eat outside?"

There was that smile again. Man.

"Sure."

They grabbed everything and moved out to a small table that sat on a teak deck overlooking the wetlands that bordered the Chesapeake Bay.

"How did you ever snag this place? I thought only millionaires lived like this."

Ian had to laugh. "Pays to be in the federal government sometimes—criminals get arrested, their assets get auctioned off. I picked this up for a song."

"Hmm. Nice deal."

Ian marveled at how normal it all felt to be sitting there with Sage, enjoying a quiet dinner. And he caught himself—it shouldn't feel normal. He shouldn't let it.

"You and EJ did some good work today."

"Oh…thanks. I didn't think you were all that hot on my work."

It was hard to tell in the evening light, but he thought his faint praise brought some color to her cheeks. He knew he'd been a bastard for most of the day and he didn't know why he was feeling so soft toward her now. Scratch that—he did know. He just didn't like admitting it.

"I'm not—not about your writing viruses or being involved with Locke. But one of my, um, consultants told me Locke often does what you said—uses his underlings—" he chose to avoid the word *groupies* that Sarah had actually used "—to do his dirty work. I guess that sounds like what happened to you."

Sage stared at him intensely, and he frowned, wondering why, but didn't say anything. She did.

"Does that mean…you believe me?"

Ian shrugged, not really knowing how much to give away. "I'm willing to admit there is a chance that you were not the programmer of that virus. But as you said, you still sent it out. And it still did do a lot of harm."

Her shoulders sagged a little. "True."

"But it's in the past."

Her eyes raised to his again. "Yes."

Taking a deep breath, he stood, walking to the rail and staring out over the water. After a few moments he realized she'd joined him, standing only a few inches away.

"You had a good time today."

Her brow furrowed. She seemed confused by his comment, so he elaborated.

"With EJ. Working on the code. It must have been like old times. You want back in."

He felt more than saw her pull back from him, her chin kissing up as it always did when she was settling in for a fight.

"Don't try to trap me, Ian, asking questions like that."

"But it's true, isn't it?"

"Not the way you think. I do want to return to working with computers in some professional—and *legal*—capacity. I love it and I'm good at it. Do you think the desire to do it just goes away?"

"It should, perhaps, after what you've gone through. Or maybe even if you still want it, you shouldn't get too close. I'm surprised you're so eager, really, to find that kind of work."

She expelled a frustrated breath. "Ian, it's not like being an alcoholic. I'll never work on viruses again, not

in terms of writing them. But I would be good at pre-
vention work, security. I know I would be."

"Kind of like a drug addict using legal drugs to get
their fix."

Her jaw set again.

"That's ridiculous. It's a talent I have. It's what I
know. Do you just expect me to work at useless jobs
for the rest of my life?"

"You could reeducate. Be something else. A
teacher."

"I have absolutely no urge to teach unless it's computer science. I want to work with technology. There's
nothing else I love as much."

She turned to him, her hand closing around his arm,
somehow physically urging him to understand. "Besides, I was a kid back then. Impressionable. Stupid. I
admit that, but I'm not either of those things now. And
you know, maybe working from the right side of the
law, I can help prevent some computer crimes from
happening. Make up for what I did before."

"And will that be enough, Sage? Won't you secretly
be dying for more? To push past the boundaries, to test
the limits? Isn't that more your style?"

The air crackled between them, and he was incredibly aware of that delicate but strong hand on his arm.
Desire rocked through him and just became more intense as she edged closer, a wicked dare in her gaze.

"Are you asking me that? Or yourself? Maybe we're
two of a kind—both wanting something we aren't sup-

posed to have. Intoxicating, isn't it?" She moved her fingers over his skin ever so slightly. "Aren't *you* secretly dying for more, Ian? Don't you want to cross the line again? Afraid to let yourself, though, aren't you?" She moved a step closer, looking up into his face. "Afraid to let yourself have me?"

He stepped back quickly, pulling his arm back as if it had been burned.

"You're a game player, aren't you, sweetheart?"

"No more so than yourself. We're more alike than you think."

"Right. This afternoon you were all over EJ—the two of you like peas in a pod. I guess it's the man of the moment for you, whoever can get you where you need to go? You'll do me if I don't arrest you. Would you do EJ just as easily if he gets you a job? Then who's next?"

He waited a second for her response, fully expecting fur to fly, and he was surprised when she remained silent, looking out at the water for a few minutes before she returned her steady, knowing gaze to his, her jade eyes alight with realization, almost amazement.

"That sounds like jealousy, Ian."

He was taken aback. "Jealousy? Hardly."

She stepped forward, closing the distance between them.

"Hmm. Making hurtful comments because you don't like me sitting and laughing with another man—

a handsome man—sounds like jealousy to me." She placed her hand on his cheek, trailing his soft fingers along it. "But don't worry. I'm all yours. If you want me."

6

SAGE HELD HER BREATH, saw the tense muscle in his jaw twitch under her touch. He was fighting for control and she was delighting in destroying it. She wasn't nervous at all. She was unexplainably giddy. Having evaded arrest and being here alone with Ian, a sense of power shivered through her, stoking her own desire, daring her to tempt him to the limit.

She might not know what made Ian tick, but she knew how to get under his skin. She forgot everything else except finding her way in, her mind in predatory mode. She knew she could have him. And thank God, because she wanted him more than she wanted her next breath.

He kept trying to push her away, trying to make what they were sharing cheap and ugly, but she wouldn't let him. There was magic in the air, whether he wanted to admit it or not. She smiled, marveling at the feeling of his skin beneath her fingers, taut and warm, freshly shaved. His hand came up, capturing hers.

"You're playing with fire, Sage."

"Uh-huh."

His hand tightened on hers and his other arm hooked around the small of her back, pulling her none too gently up against him. She bit back a tiny moan when she felt the long, hard length of him against her stomach and raised her free arm around his neck, lifting her face to his, bringing their faces close, their lips just a breath away from touching.

"You want me, Ian. You may not want to, but you do." She lifted her eyes, meeting his, studying the indecision reflected in his expression. She smiled, pressing her mouth to his gently, punctuating each word with a small butterfly kiss. "Let…me…make…it…easy…for…you."

On the last kiss she darted her tongue out, dragging it sensuously along his lower lip. Before she could slide it back in the other direction, he consumed her. Any coherent thought she had went up in the flames of his passionate response.

She thought she was controlling the game, playing on her terms, but his crushing kiss stole her breath and her sense of controlling anything—Ian, herself, the situation. Suddenly everything was out of control and she didn't care. Control was vastly overrated when a man like this had his hands all over you with such hunger that he couldn't seem to get enough.

His lips left hers and trailed a searing path down her neckline, his tongue tasting her skin, and she arched back to allow him better access as her entire body came alive.

God, she hadn't felt like this in her life. Maybe it was because she was a woman now, grown and ready, or maybe it was Ian, but she was so gloriously on fire she could barely think. He pushed up her dress and slid his hand along her body to her breasts. He rolled one nipple between his thumb and forefinger while his mouth latched over the other. She cried out, the sensation was so intense.

She wound her hands into his hair, holding him close and keeping herself upright as the onslaught continued. The dampness between her legs became a hot slick of desire, and she tried to tell him what she needed, but each word she attempted to utter was lost in a fresh wave of sensation.

They were bent around each other on the patio like an erotic wood carving she had once seen, two figures entwined so that you couldn't tell where one started and other ended. Dusk settled around them and all that could be seen from their vantage point on the deck were some boats on the Chesapeake. If those boaters happened to have binoculars, they were sure getting a show tonight.

The idea that someone could be watching added one more layer to her excitement, and Sage wiggled suggestively, not feeling one shred of self-consciousness as Ian pushed her panties down and out of the way. He looked up at her, his hands rubbing along the outsides of her calves and thighs and along her bottom, his skin ruddy with desire, his pupils dilated as he took in her partially naked form. His voice was rough with need, and she felt his breath on her skin, making her shiver.

"We should go inside. It isn't as private as it seems out here." He glanced briefly toward the water and then back at her. She smiled, shaking her head. Lifting her arms up, she peeled off her dress, baring herself to the night air and his eyes.

"No one's looking, Ian. And if they are, so what? We'll give them something to talk about."

IAN WASN'T SURE HE WAS as crazy about potentially having an audience as Sage apparently was, but what was more important was that he was next to a gloriously naked woman, ripe and ready for the taking. He wasn't about to get into a debate about location.

The shadows were cloaking them somewhat, he reassured himself as he investigated the taste of the skin at the meeting of hip and thigh. As he tasted more, he increasingly lost any self-consciousness about where he was. All he knew was that he wanted Sage, and for the moment all bets were off. If she wanted to stay out there in the open, he wasn't about to argue.

He felt her quiver under his hands as he lightly traced his fingertips along the backs of her legs, across the sensitive hollows behind her knees, up to the soft rounds of her derriere. There he let his hands slip gently into the warm crevice where skin met skin, exploring every bit of her, delving and testing into soft, secret places, smiling as his fingers prodded the tight bud he sought, penetrating ever so slightly. He felt her quiver become a shudder as she moaned in pleasure and clenched him with her strong muscles. He waited for her signal to go further, to journey more deeply, and she pressed back against him, her voice a ragged whisper.

"Ian, please, yes. More…"

He thrust gently with his finger while spanning his hand fully between her legs, his palm pressed against her sex so that his thumb could massage her swollen, slippery nub while he pressed gently inside of her. In only seconds she went to pieces.

He lifted his face and watched her come, gloried in how she let go, convulsing, leaning back to grab the rail as he kept probing and stroking until her cries died to gasps and she looked down at him, her eyes dark with pleasure, damp red curls plastered against her flushed cheeks.

He ran his hands over her skin, thrilled by her responses, her absolute lack of inhibition. She seemed still dazed from her climax, so he was slightly shocked at the clarity of her voice, the sharpness of her command.

"Take your clothes off, Ian. Now."

He looked into her flushed face and rose, yanking off his T-shirt and quickly losing his shorts, until he stood as naked as she was, his throbbing erection jutting eagerly toward her.

She looked over him slowly, and he let her, enjoying the excitement on her face. She smiled slowly and in such a sexy, feline way that his cock jerked in response, thickening with need just watching her smile. For him.

"You're a very generous lover, Ian, but you know what they say about having to get as good as you give."

"Why don't you show me?"

"Gladly."

Stepping close, she came as near as she could without touching, letting the sensual promise of the moment hang between them. Reaching out, she wrapped her fingers around his length, her eyes promising and daring him at the same time as she eased her palm up and down his shaft, caressing him. His eyes went molten, and she saw him fight giving himself over to her totally. He was keeping himself in check, and she wasn't going to have any of that. How much he could take?

She stepped a little closer, letting the tip of him prod her belly, and whispered, "The rule is you can't move. You can't touch, speak or change position. If you break the rules, I stop."

She slid down his body, dragging her tongue down the flat, supple muscles of his torso, all the while stroking him until he shuddered, but he still held his position. His breath was ragged, and she smiled against his skin.

"Mmm, you taste so good, Ian."

Mimicking his actions and running her hands up and down the length of his strong, sinewy legs, she rubbed her cheek along the hot, soft skin of his erection, nuzzling him tentatively before licking him lightly, teasingly. At the tentative touch of her tongue he went rigid and growled through clenched teeth, but he still didn't move.

Bringing her palm up to cup him, she investigated his body more thoroughly, loving the manly scent of his sex, feeling her own heart pound harder as she kissed him more insistently, finally wrapping her lips around his fullness and sliding down to the base, taking him as deeply as she could. She sighed against him when he sank his hands into her hair—somewhere in the back of her mind she supposed his move was against her rules, but she didn't care. They were far beyond the rules.

She lost track of time, licking and nipping, sucking and kissing, until he let out a loud groan of tortured ecstasy and she felt his thighs quake with the effort of maintaining control. From the hot, pulsing energy that was practically melting in her mouth, she figured he wouldn't last much longer, and though she was enjoying herself thoroughly, she wanted more. She wanted all of him.

Drawing back, she turned her head, loosening his fingers from her curls, and dragged her lips across his palm, looking up at him wordlessly. She was struck by the intense passion etched into his expression, the blatant need she saw there, the fine sheen of sweat that covered his body. He was magnificent.

His gaze locked onto hers and she just nodded silently. In a second his hands slipped under her arms, pulling her up as if she had no weight at all, and he sealed her mouth with a kiss that was steamier than she would have thought possible before turning her in front of the rail and positioning himself behind. He leaned forward, pressing against her, and she shivered. His voice was close by her ear.

"Don't move. Don't turn around. I'll be right back."

She wasn't sure what he was up to until a moment later he reemerged on the patio and she heard a ripping sound. Breathing a sigh of relief, she was glad that one of them had thought of protection. She should have known Ian would never take that kind of a chance, and for once she was glad for his never-faltering presence of mind, much as she had been trying to wreck it.

Sage wrapped her hands around the cool cast-iron railing, her body knotted in anticipation as his hands planted on her hips and his knees nudged hers, opening them wider. She helped willingly, bending slightly, offering him what they both wanted.

She closed her eyes and lifted her face to the sky, balanced on the fine edge of expectation when Ian plunged suddenly, his hardness filling her completely with one long, desperate thrust. She cried out, her hands tightening on the rail as her knees went weak with the thrill of it. She whimpered, her body happily accommodating the fullness of his and wanting more.

Deep inside her, Ian pressed his front to her back, wrapping his arms around her, covering her breasts, massaging her and leaving kisses everywhere on her neck and shoulders as he moved against her, whispering into her ear, urging her on.

She rotated her hips back against him, seeking release from the wonderful pressure that was building inside until she could hardly stand up. He felt increasingly rigid and thick inside of her, his head resting on her shoulder, their sighs of pleasure filling the humid evening air.

She hovered at the edge of climax, afraid for one brief moment she might not make it over in time. But she needn't have feared. Ian traveled one hand down her body and slid it between her thighs, flicking her lightly in exactly the right spot. The moment his fingers touched her she unraveled. Her climax rippled through her, and she lost all sense of anything but Ian filling her, his body stroking hers. She lost all control, grinding wildly against him as he thrust into her with increasing speed until he also yelled out as his climax shook through him.

Ian tried to catch his breath. Had he ever felt this way with a woman? Not in recent memory. Not even with his wife had he ever experienced such insanely strong pleasure. Sage's skin was hot and moist next to his, and he locked his arms around her, touching her everywhere, not able to get enough.

He didn't want to leave her body. He didn't want the separateness between them that was inevitable, didn't want to lose the moment and travel back into a reality that was becoming more confusing by the second.

So he held on, wrapped her against him, buried inside her until his softening erection left him no choice. Still he held her, unsure of how to deal with the intensity of what had just happened between them. He tried to stem the thoughts rising to the surface as his mind cleared, but they wouldn't be stopped.

Why now? Why her? How could he let himself lose control like this and what was he going to do about it?

He sighed, burying his face in the back of her neck, letting himself soak up the intoxicating scents of her body.

And then he let go.

He stepped back and watched her straighten, her back still to him. He had no idea what to say but just reached for his shorts. Pulling them on, he looked up and saw her still nude, watching him. He swallowed, averting his eyes. In spite of what they'd just experienced, the sight of her sent a fresh wave of lust slamming into him unexpectedly.

"Uh, you might want to get dressed."

Her eyes gave nothing away and she said nothing. He felt increasingly awkward, so he picked her dress up from the patio floor and shook it out.

"I'm sorry if this was ruined. I can get it cleaned for you."

Something sparked in her eyes but was quickly hidden as she reached for the dress and took it from his hand, though she didn't put it on. She walked by him, her voice nonchalant.

"Don't worry about it."

As she walked calmly into the house and up the stairs to her room, Ian pushed his hands through his hair. Though he hated to admit it, he was very worried.

LOCKE LOWERED HIS binoculars and spat over the side of the rail into the water. His breath was ragged with anger as well as desire and the two blended into an ugly mix. If LadyBug was faking it, she was putting in one hell of a performance.

He'd watched her undress for the fed, her body fuller now in womanhood, hotter than he'd remembered, and his hands had clenched so tightly onto the eyeglasses he'd almost snapped them in half.

The sailboat he was "borrowing" for the weekend— he'd hacked into the marina's Web site and made a few "adjustments" so there had been no questions asked when he'd shown up to take it out on the water— bobbed gently on the calm surface of the Chesapeake. It was a clear night, and he'd had no problem at all see- ing the cop's house from his vantage point on the water.

When his LadyBug had bent over the patio rail and let the cop do her, Locke had gone hard himself, all of the passion they'd once shared rushing to the surface. He knew he needed an outlet for it before he went crazy. His voice was rough and commanding, his eyes never leaving the spot where the couple he'd watched was no doubt still going at it even though he couldn't see any- thing in detail.

"Candace. Come here."

He waited for less than a minute, but it seemed like forever, his frustration and anger simmering to a boil. Was LadyBug playing the cop? Or was she playing him? How would he be able to know?

He wouldn't—not until he met her. Looked into her

face. Buried himself inside her. Then he would know. And if she was playing him...

Candace, his companion for the weekend, stepped beside him. It was more convincing—and less threatening—when he'd shown up to get the boat as part of a couple. The guy working at the marina had handed it over with no problem. Although the paperwork the marina had on file had noted the owner was not slated to pick up the boat for another week, the guy trusted the computer's online schedule, which said differently. Locke laughed to himself about what a breeze it had been, running his hand along the stern rail—it was some luxury vessel.

He turned to face Candace, raking his eyes over her bikini-clad form as she stared flirtatiously up at him. He'd picked her up on campus; she was effortlessly seduced by a handsome older guy who was looking to party on his private boat for the weekend. She was all of twenty—the same age LadyBug had been when he'd met her. But Candace was far more experienced and sophisticated than LadyBug had ever been. She was happy to use him and was willing to be used, which was convenient.

"I need you." Reaching forward, he pulled roughly at the thin material of the bikini, ripping it off. She laughed and stepped closer. Kissing her hard, he reached down, freeing his erection. He dug his hands into the ample breasts that she pressed against him, thinking about how she was much larger than his baby girl but satisfying all the same.

Remembering how LadyBug had gone at it with the cop on the patio as he'd watched, her passionate expression as the fed had thrust into her from behind, Locke spun Candace around and pushed her up against the rail, ripping the bikini bottoms off and bending her over, pushing inside where she was already hot and ready for him. Apparently she didn't need much finesse, which was good. He didn't want to seduce her, after all, he wanted to screw her.

Candace's cries of release and enjoyment blurred for him as he closed his eyes, reliving the sight of Lady-Bug's ripe mouth formed in passionate cries. He jack-hammered himself into Candace's tight heat, his breath ragged with the memory. He let all of his anger and frustration pound into the body in front of him and he was barely conscious of the young woman, who was no doubt putting on one of her best performances.

All he wanted to do was release what he'd felt watching someone else have the only woman he'd really wanted for the last five years. As his climax blasted through him, he yelled out over the water, one name repeating through his mind as the pleasure drained him: LadyBug.

SAGE CLOSED THE DOOR behind her with a heavy sigh, sagging back against it. God, that was hard. Walking away when all she really wanted was to be with him again. Trying to pretend his pulling away from her didn't matter. Facing the night alone.

It mattered. But he couldn't know that. She'd been

saved by the fact that he couldn't see the shock of loss she knew must have shown on her face. She was grateful she'd had a few moments to compose herself before she'd faced him.

She hadn't expected it either, the rush of emotions that had swamped her when he'd held her so tightly against him after they'd peaked, his heart thudding strongly against the hollow of her back, his face pressed into her neck. Even if Ian didn't mean it in an emotional way, how he'd held her meant something. To her, anyway.

But she'd seen the regret in his expression when she did face him—it was clear he wasn't feeling anything more than that. Not that she had expected more. She knew the score; he'd been straight with her. She knew he was sorry about losing control and she tried to find some satisfaction in that. It's what she'd wanted, right? To make him lose control? To keep him off balance?

Somehow it didn't help all that much. He'd lost control, but he'd gotten it back quickly. She hovered on the edge of losing something much more threatening.

Walking to the shower, she shook off the sense of hurt and loneliness. She couldn't expect him to love her—or even to like her, for that matter. But she could make him want her. She'd driven him to the edge and a tingle formed at the base of her spine when she realized she wanted to do it again.

If all she could have was his body, she could live with that. She had to remember what was important. As long as her freedom was part of the package. Three more days to go. Three days to be with Ian. Three days to find Locke. Turning a hot stream of water on full blast, she stepped under it and let it wash over her. Three days until her life could begin all over again.

"I DIDN'T EXPECT YOU BACK SO SOON."

"Yeah, sorry for the late call. I just don't want to waste time and thought you might have found something."

EJ nodded and grabbed two beers from the fridge, eyeing Ian speculatively as he stood in the middle of the kitchen pacing like a caged animal.

"Millie's sound asleep, but let's go outside, just in case. I gave her the shorthand version this afternoon. I don't want her getting concerned."

"Sure. She looks great. The wedding is soon?"

EJ nodded, and Ian thought he saw his friend's features tense slightly. "Six months."

"Sounds like she's neck-deep in preparations and trying to pull you down, too. Did you try to convince her to elope?"

EJ snorted. "Like that would ever happen. This is going to be the event of the year. Damn it, Ian, I think she has white horses or some insane thing like that lined up."

Ian barked out a laugh and put a sympathetic hand on EJ's shoulder.

"I'm here for you, man. We'll have a rockin' bachelor party—best man duties and all. No white horses, I promise."

EJ sighed. "Thanks. Where's Sage?"

"Home."

"You just left her there?"

"I locked her room. From the outside."

"Jesus, Ian. That's kind of a shitty thing to do."

Ian narrowed his gaze, irked at the response. "What would you know about it, Ethan? You think she's a goddamn hero."

EJ cocked his head, appearing unbothered by Ian's outburst. "No, I don't think that and you know it. But she's not hacking anymore and she needs someone to help her get a new start. That really should be your job, right?"

"No, my job is to try to keep her out of trouble and to arrest her if she breaks the law again."

EJ shrugged. "She is trying to help, after all. There's no reason to bark at her all the time. You have to admit she's a pretty little thing and kind of sweet. That red hair—"

Ian might have growled, but he wasn't sure, as the next moment EJ burst into knowing laughter, setting his beer down on the table.

"I thought so."

Ian did growl this time. "You thought what?"

"You're completely gone for her, aren't you?"

"Hardly. She's in my custody. Off-limits."

"Right. But desire, love, all those messy emotions don't usually play by the rules, my friend. And she is a beautiful woman. Smart, too."

"I don't love her, if that's what you're thinking."

EJ nodded, pursing his lips thoughtfully. "Okay. You've slept with her, though?"

Ian looked away but nodded. He and EJ had known each other too long for him to lie about it.

"I would hate to be you, man, when you go back there. You sleep with a woman and then lock her in her room and leave? She didn't strike me as one to take something like that easily."

"It's not like that. She won't care. We have an… arrangement."

EJ's expression cooled a little.

"I never knew you to use a woman like that, Ian. Especially one you're supposed to be protecting."

The barb hit, and it stuck in a very sore spot. He wasn't about to let this conversation go any further. Leaving his beer on the table, he met EJ's gaze head-on.

"I'm not protecting her. I protect society from her."

"It goes both ways and you know it."

He did know it and he chose to ignore it. This wasn't the conversation he'd come here for. "Did you find anything more on the disk?"

EJ's eyebrows arched at the cool dismissal the change of subject signaled. "As a matter of fact, yeah."

"What?"

"Bread crumbs. Locke left a path of clues for Sage— little bits of information that were coded into the notations, things that don't mean much to me but might make sense to her."

"A location? Where to find him?"

"Maybe. You're going to have to let her look through it."

Ian nodded. "Okay. We'll do it tomorrow."

"You mentioned earlier today there was something else you wanted to talk to me about?"

Ian blinked, trying to remember. "Oh, yeah. I wanted to ask you to think about joining HotWires."

EJ was clearly surprised, and it showed.

"The NPD team? But I'm not a cop."

"You worked for DOJ. You have investigative skills, background. And you have computer skills. I don't need just any cop, I need cops who can do the stuff you do at a keyboard."

"Well, yeah, but my work for the Justice Department was a while ago."

Ian moved forward. "You're a good lawyer and you're a magician, EJ, as a programmer. Your experience with fraud investigation would be valuable to the team. You know how to look at code in a ways other people don't even think about, and I need that. I know you've been restless with the family business for a few years now. This could be a good change."

"Maybe. But I do have family obligations. They'd be pretty ticked if I quit. And to be honest, they've needed me here since Dad died. I don't know how I could work two positions. I could still freelance for you, like I'm doing now. I'm always happy to help."

Ian shook his head, knowing he was putting EJ in a tough spot, but he wanted to push it. He knew his friend, and not only would EJ be an excellent addition to the team, Ian knew he hadn't been happy in the family business for a long time.

"I want you full-time. You were a lot happier when you worked for DOJ. You could do some good work here, EJ. Your skills are going to waste. Your dad's been gone for a while, the company is on its feet now…."

EJ still seemed to be processing what Ian was asking, and nodded. "Can I think about it? I don't think Millie will be thrilled with the idea, but I'll run it by her. I need to at least do that, since my decision would affect her, too."

"Okay, but you need to decide quickly. I want to get the team up and running."

EJ nodded, standing, and the two men walked to the back door. Ian stopped in the doorway, looking back at his friend.

"For what it's worth, EJ, I'm not using her. Not like you think."

"Then what are you doing?"

Ian shook his head, looking out into the dark front yard, the fragrant flowers on the porch reminding him of Sage's scent. "Damned if I know."

EJ refrained from further comment, though his eyes seemed to soften a bit. He put his hand out, and Ian shook it firmly.

"You'll let me know soon about the job?"

"Yeah. See you tomorrow."

WHEN HE RETURNED TO THE house, Ian didn't even bother turning on the lights but went directly upstairs.

He unlocked Sage's door when he passed by her room on the way to his own. Everything was silent; she must have been sleeping for hours now. She wouldn't have even known he'd locked it.

In a way he felt let down. He was exhausted but wired from no sleep and too much tension and would have felt better if she'd been waiting for him on the other side of the door, spitting mad and spoiling for a fight. He stood outside the door for a moment, shaking his head in self-derision. He wanted her again. Wanted nothing more than to open that door and slip into her bed and her body, emptying himself until there was nothing left. And he knew if he did that, he'd be lost.

7

SAGE FELT IAN'S GAZE burning into her skin as she tried to concentrate on the screen. In spite of their passionate lovemaking the night before and the relaxed conversation that had existed for a few precious moments during supper, he was back to watching her as if she was apt to bolt away at any moment. She just tried to ignore him as she worked, but his presence and those looming looks were difficult to block out.

Ian was reading through a report he'd received on Locke—she'd been asking him a question and had seen the e-mail attachment pop up on his computer. She knew the report wouldn't offer up much. Locke was careful.

Her fingers tapped the keyboard. At first it felt awkward—it had been a while since she'd sat at a computer—but soon her hands flew over the keys and the excitement of it thrilled her. She glanced over her shoulder at Ian. Not that she could let on about how good it felt, especially given the situation and the subject matter. Locke had indeed left her coded messages, broken up like parts of a puzzle and scattered through his notations, and she was trying to put them all together.

EJ had described them as "bread crumbs," just as in the fairy tale, and that's exactly how it was. But she felt as if this particular path was going to lead her farther into the woods instead of safely back home. She wrinkled her brow, focusing on the task at hand.

"I've got it—the first one anyway. He is giving me locations, but I think they are clues, not the place where he actually is. He wants me to figure it out, to hack my way to him. Typical."

"Where is it?" Ian was immediately at her side, scrutinizing the screen.

Sage bit her lip, taking a deep breath. The first location was a set of map coordinates that she plugged into a GPS site, recognizing the place immediately. It was a secluded spot where she and Locke had once made love. Where they had first made love. She didn't want to share that information with Ian, particularly.

"It's a small, deserted island on the Intracoastal."

"Do you think he has set up shop there?"

She shook her head. "No, it's wild land. I'll have to figure out the other ones to get a whole picture. He's not just going to come out and tell me where he is, Ian. Locke is never that direct. Besides, he knows someone else could hack the code and find him, so these are just clues not actual locations. It's probably a triangulation or a puzzle of some kind."

Ian sighed heavily and paced to the other side of the room. EJ had left them alone, needing to go in to the office for a few hours, and Sage had been chipping away at the code since he'd left.

"How long will it take you to decipher the others?"

"Hopefully not long. EJ did the hard part, finding all the pieces. If he got them all, it's just a matter of decoding and figuring out what he's trying to tell me."

"We don't have much time. If he plans on setting this virus loose in two days, we need to find him fast."

Sage didn't respond but just tapped at the keys more furiously, grumping. She was getting hungry, but Ian never seemed to think about sleep or food—those were afterthoughts. Work was his main priority.

"If I didn't know better, I'd think you were a robot or something."

He stood by the window and turned to look at her. "What's that supposed to mean?"

"You never stop. You are so focused on work, you don't even stop to go to the bathroom or eat. Don't you ever just get tired?"

"We're working against the clock here, Sage. I can't afford to get tired." He ran a hand over his face, seeming to struggle to remain patient, and then set his hands on his hips, regarding her. "Are you hungry?"

"Yes."

"I'll get something. You keep working."

"Are you going out?"

Maybe her tone was a little too hopeful, because his eyes narrowed and suspicion entered his gaze again. He shook his head. "No. I'm sure EJ has something. Just keep at it. I'll be in the kitchen."

Sage's shoulders slumped and all of a sudden the fun of working through the clues faded. She couldn't quite make sense of the moods running rampant over her. That morning, when Ian had told her she was going to be able to work on the code, she'd been excited but nervous. She'd wondered if she'd even be able to do the basics anymore, but that was no problem. It had come back quickly.

And it had been fun, until Ian's glares and hovering had gotten on her nerves, and then she'd just wanted to be done. That was frustrating. But while EJ had done the grunt work of finding all the encrypted nuggets of code, putting them back together was not only tedious but it gave her time to think, to remember things about her past that were better forgotten.

Locke was playing games with her, toying with her yet again, leading her along like some hapless child. And to be reminded of their affair, of the things they'd done on that island and elsewhere, was deflating. And she'd been down long enough—she wanted to rise up. It wasn't going to be easy, though, from the looks of it.

Being sandwiched between her past broken up to bits on the screen and Ian's harsh attitude toward her in the present was getting to her. He hadn't so much as touched her or even acknowledged what had happened between them since they'd awakened that morning.

Though she hated to admit it, it made her feel cheap. And that made her angry—she didn't expect wine and roses, but some acknowledgement that she was a human being would be nice. When she'd made a sarcastic comment about it not being necessary to lock her in her room at night, he'd just looked away. The dismissal had hurt as much as his blatant distrust.

So she had two men dorking around with her, and both of them held her future in the balance. Instead of gaining more control over her life, she just seemed to be spinning more out of control.

She attacked the keyboard with a fury, her fingers flying and her concentration so intense she didn't even notice Ian setting a plate down at her side.

"Here. Take a break."

She looked at the fruits, cheese and crackers arranged on the china plate and the sparkling, cold glass of iced tea with the little wedge of lemon and mint. He'd fixed this—for her?

All of her irritation was washed away in her overemotional response to so small a gesture. Sure, he was only feeding her because she complained, and it wasn't *that* big of a deal, but... God, what was wrong with her today? She felt her eyes sting and wiped her hand across them, hoping he didn't see.

But he did. As usual, Ian saw everything.

"What's wrong? I know it's more of a snack than a lunch, but it will have to do until—"

Sage shook her head, turning around quickly to interrupt. "No, it's lovely. Really. I guess I'm just a little tense. And this was so nice of you. It almost looks too pretty to eat, you went through such trouble to fix it all so nicely—"

Ian stared at her as if she was losing her mind, which she very well might be. "It's just fruit, Sage."

She nodded, feeling more ridiculous by the moment, and reached down to pluck a cherry from the plate.

"It was kind of you nonetheless. I appreciate it. I was starving."

He said nothing in response as she popped the fruit into her mouth, but she was aware of him studying her.

"And you don't expect kindness from me, do you?" He ran his hand through his hair. "I guess I can't blame you. I've been a prick of epic proportions lately. I'm sorry about that."

She shrugged while darting her tongue out to catch some juice that dribbled down when she bit into a slice of peach. "No, you're not sorry. It's just your job, right?"

Sage was intrigued by the change in his demeanor. He crossed the room and reached down to pick up some cheese from the plate.

"No, I am. There's a lot of stress right now, but it's really not my job to be on your case every minute. You've made it clear you're trying to help. It's also not part of my job to—"

"Have sex with me?" she said baldly, and he hesitated, then nodded. She could tell he felt uncomfortable with the casual way she'd completed his sentence.

"I just want to get this guy and get this over with. For both of our sakes."

She took the glass of iced tea, swallowing deeply, trying to remove the hard lump that had formed in her throat. When Ian saw the look on her face, he stepped forward, placing his hand on her arm, forcing her to lower the tea. Her hand shook as she set it back on the table. What a mess she was.

"Sage, I didn't mean that how it sounded. Or I don't know, maybe I did…."

His voice turned oddly gentle, just confusing her more. Why was he being so nice to her *now?* His harshness was easier to deal with.

"It's okay, Ian, I know the score—"

He tipped her chin up. His mouth was drawn tight, and there was something in his eyes she didn't recognize, and it disturbed her.

"No, I don't think you do. You're tough, Sage, but we both have a lot at stake."

"I'm not worried about it," she lied and her breath caught in her chest.

He was silent for a moment and then lowered his head. She sucked in a breath, unprepared for the sudden move. His lips brushed across hers, teasing her. She let out the breath and he captured it, sliding his hands into her hair, nestling her against him while his mouth played over hers in the most tender, seductive kiss she'd ever experienced.

The kiss was undeniably hot, so sexual she simmered as he licked and nibbled, teasing her mouth open so he could explore further. She moaned against him, wrapping her arms around him, pressing herself into him. Of all the things she'd felt today, this was undeniably the best.

His mouth left hers, traveled across her cheek to

nuzzle her ear. She was sure she would come on the spot from the sensations that were shooting through her.

He whispered, "You taste sweet, like cherries, peaches and honey, and all I want is more," before he returned to her mouth, continuing the same seductive onslaught he had started.

Sage's head spun. She had no idea what was happening but clung to him, hungry for more of this gentle heat. She felt him harden against her belly and she reached down to stroke him, pushing their embrace toward what she assumed would be the natural progression of things. But he surprised her yet again by capturing her hand and just holding it while he continued kissing her.

When he finally lifted his head, his expression was alive with desire but also softened by a gentler emotion. She had no idea what to do. Finally she spoke, trying to figure it out.

"Do you want to go upstairs?"

Ian shook his head, looking so deeply into her eyes she felt the urge to hide away somewhere and not let him see too much. But instead she stood frozen, looking back at him.

"No, Sage. I want you, you know that. And we'll probably have each other again sooner rather than later. But I've been hard on you. And I guess I just wanted you to know, to realize—" he faltered and glanced away for a moment, looking unsure "—that sometimes it can be tender and good and slow. And sweet. You are worth those things, even though I haven't shown you that."

Sage's head was really spinning. What on earth was he saying to her? What had brought on this sudden change? Was he doing this to confuse her? Throw her off balance?

It was working. She couldn't think. She stepped away, breaking their eye contact.

"I should, uh, get back to work."

He nodded. She could still feel his eyes on her when she started tapping at the keys again, but now it was distracting in an entirely different way.

SAGE SAT BACK IN FRONT of the computer, effectively erasing his presence. It wasn't so easy for him—he still wanted to touch her, to continue what they'd started, but he fought the impulse.

Maybe he'd stopped because they were in EJ's home and his friend's words about using Sage pricked at his conscience, reminding him that he and Sage could never be together—not really. But also because she was still a woman. And she deserved to be treated like one.

The problem was, when he allowed himself to start thinking like that, other thoughts followed. Dangerous thoughts. Impossible thoughts. Thoughts he hadn't had about any woman in a long time. Thoughts he couldn't have about *this* woman.

He saw her back tense slightly and realized he was still staring. All he wanted was to close the space between them and touch her again, but instead he turned away and got back to the report on Locke.

Sarah had been thorough, but there wasn't much to

tell. Some discussion about his coding at a Web site, nothing too useful. Apparently Locke kept to himself and communicated via a number of pseudonyms, so he was nearly impossible to track.

Sarah had located several bank accounts, none of them showing suspicious balances or any recent activity. There were a few virus incidents, fairly severe ones, that local authorities and hacking groupies attributed to Locke, but no one had any evidence. He read through an FBI report on one of the incidents. The man arrested claimed to have been working with Locke but had no proof. Just like Sage. Ian felt a wave of guilt settle over him.

Locke was sitting quietly, waiting to implement his plan. Waiting for Sage. But Ian was going to make sure that whatever he was up to this time, it wasn't going to work.

SEVERAL HOURS LATER Sage looked up when EJ walked in. Eyeing them, he threw a stack of mail on the table and hung his coat neatly over a chair. He was in full business armor, and while she'd never been one to go for guys in suits, EJ packed a wallop when he dressed up.

She wasn't one for swooning, but she appreciated a good-looking man when she saw one, especially when her eyes and back ached after sitting at the computer for over eight hours. He was literally a sight for sore eyes. She also looked forward to seeing him because he was always nice to her. EJ smiled at both of them and took a seat.

"You guys still at it? You're in the same exact position I left you in. Did you even stop for food?"

Ian nodded toward the empty pizza box on the table, and EJ arched a brow.

"Well, while it may be a stretch to call that food exactly, I guess it's something. So where are we with the code? Did you find out what those bits were about?" He looked at Sage inquiringly.

"I think I have it."

Both men came forward to see what was on the screen. Ian looked tired, she noticed. Not that he would admit it.

"Have what?"

"Locke's location. Or at least the spot he seems to be leading me to."

"Where?"

"There's a college bar near Virginia Beach, the Blue Shark. You wouldn't know it, it's just a local dive. We used to go there all the time because you could stay all night, drink on the cheap and no one really paid attention to what you were doing."

"And you think that's it? Can you be sure?"

"As sure as these clues have led me to believe. So now I guess all I have to do is meet him, right?"

EJ spoke up. "It doesn't seem like a great idea for you to go in there alone. He could be dangerous."

Sage arched an eyebrow. "Well, I'm the one he's contacting—and I can tell you he wouldn't like me showing up with another guy. Besides, if he knows about my sentence, where I am, then he knows about Ian. It's not exactly a secret that you've run my life for the last five years. So how else exactly do you plan to get close to him? You have to rely on me."

"Is there any way to tell from those clues what he wants?"

Sage's face flamed and she broke eye contact. She had a pretty good idea what Locke wanted with her and how he would expect her to show her loyalty. She didn't have to say another word, and Ian stiffened.

"He'll want you to sleep with him."

Sage nodded.

"Are you willing to do that?"

Tension crackled in the air, and Sage met Ian's eyes, her voice steady though she felt as if there was an earthquake going on inside of her. "No. But there has to be a way around it. We can stall him somehow. Though resuming our…old relationship—or at least leading him to believe we will—might be the only way to get him to take me to where the main computer is."

Ian was silent, staring out the window. A storm was rolling in, and a huge bolt of lightning sizzled through the sky. The loud clap of thunder that followed didn't even make him blink.

"Ian?"

He turned his head back to look at Sage, his eyes intense. Sage could tell he was forming a plan.

"I think you're onto something with leading him on. This guy has an ego the size of Godzilla, right?"

Sage snorted indelicately. "Bigger."

"That's his weakness. And you—and the fact that he wants you in his bed. But what if you were to offer him something even better?"

Sage blinked, unsure what he meant. "Like what?"

"Two of you—two beautiful women, ready to meet his every desire."

Sage's forehead furrowed. She couldn't see exactly where Ian was heading with this, but it was sounding kind of kinky. He turned to EJ, excited.

"I know a woman—Sarah Jessup—a knockout and a crack programmer. She's helped us out a lot, and I've been thinking about adding her on as a HotWires investigator. She could go in with Sage, pretending to be a new friend, and that would protect Sage from having to go back with Locke right away. The two women could offer to meet him at his house. You and I could follow."

EJ perched his chin on his tanned, groomed fingers, nodding thoughtfully. "Could work. What man is going to refuse an offer like that?"

Sage chimed in. "Locke is paranoid to a degree you can't even imagine. He won't trust anyone new, no matter how much of a knockout. He won't even trust me."

Ian smirked. "I think you are underestimating the male libido and the fantasy of having two women at the same time, sweetheart. Besides, he'll probably assume he has it all under control. His type always does."

Rain started pelting the windows, and EJ stood, speaking to Ian.

"This sounds like a workable plan, but you'd have to get your girl—uh, Sarah, was it?—up here by tomorrow. Possible?"

"Yeah. She'll do it. I'll call her, but I'm sure she'll do it."

Nodding, EJ cast a glance at the clock on the wall. "It's going to be a late one tonight then. Why don't you call her and make arrangements and you two can stay here tonight, and Sarah can meet us in the morning. There are bound to be some red-eye flights available from the city to here. I can pick her up."

Ian nodded. "I'll call her now, set it up." He met Sage's eyes, and she marveled at how his tired look had changed, sparked by the excitement of the hunt. Sage realized that Locke and Ian were in some ways different sides of the same coin: both driven to control whatever situation they were in and both predators at heart. And both had been able to breach her defenses. The thought made her shiver as he continued.

"You're willing to go along with this? You're going to have to convince him that you and Sarah are friends—friendly enough to want to get into bed with him. But EJ and I won't be far away and we'll be monitoring the whole thing. We won't let anything go wrong. All we have to do is bring him down and get to that computer in time."

Sage looked up and met his eyes calmly. "I'm ready. I can do it."

Ian nodded. "Let's get to work, then."

HOURS LATER THE WOMAN named Sarah was on her way to Norfolk, and Ian had left EJ's to return to the office to get some surveillance equipment. Sage was a little surprised he'd left her there on her own. She supposed EJ was acting as watchdog. Sitting curled up in a comfy chair by the window, watching the storm ebb, Sage was so wired she was unable to even think about sleep. She didn't hear EJ come into the room behind her.

"How about a drink? I make a mean martini."

She looked up and smiled. "I've never had a martini."

"You're in for a treat then."

While EJ worked some magic at the marble-topped bar that was tucked into the corner of the room, Sage sighed and bent down to look through a stack of books—no, not books, photo albums—that were piled on a shelf near her chair. Picking one volume up, she looked at EJ as he approached her with their drinks.

"Is it okay if I look at these?"

"Sure, that volume has no embarrassing naked baby pictures, so feel free, " he said, placing her martini on the table and then sitting across from her in an old leather wing chair.

Sage chuckled and took a sip of her drink, rolling her eyes back at the spicy taste of the drink. "Oh, this is marvelous. Do all martinis taste like this?"

EJ smiled proudly. "No, just mine. There are a lot of different martinis nowadays, but this one is a classic— except for the secret ingredient I throw in."

"Really? What is it?" She took another sip and felt more relaxed by the moment.

"Well, that's a secret."

She grinned. She felt so at ease around EJ, it was nice. "Hmm. Where's your fiancée tonight?"

"She's staying at her mother's until tomorrow. Some wedding preparations seem to take more energy than my feeble male mind can imagine, and they expect to be awake long into the night."

Sage grinned. "Sounds like it will be quite the event. My sister's wedding was like that." Sage leaned forward as if sharing a funny joke with EJ, who chuckled when she said, "She had swans. A dozen of them. Can you believe it? For the pond in the background of their pictures. Of course, no one could get near the pond because of the, uh, swan poo."

EJ chuckled, but Sage thought he seemed slightly uncomfortable all of a sudden, as if she had brought up something he would rather not discuss. Odd, she thought, for a man about to be married not to want to talk about weddings, but she turned her attention back to the albums.

Paging through the carefully preserved photos, she asked questions, commented on clothes and the striking people who filled the volume, listening with rapt interest to EJ's explanation of each picture she pointed out.

Their drinks were empty, and he pulled his chair a little closer, pointing to a man in a black-and-white photograph standing beside a huge boat on the shores of the Elizabeth.

"That's my granddad. Standing by the first boat his factory ever made in 1901, that tug. It's still going, though they just use it for river tours now. He progressed onto much bigger ships, and fast."

"He's so handsome. You resemble him—but I'm glad you don't have the mustache." They laughed and she inquired further. "So you work for your family's business? Have you always?"

He sighed. "Feels like it sometimes. But no, I didn't work here always. I studied law in college, like Dad and Granddad, but I started out working for the government as an investigator with the Department of Justice."

"Why'd you quit?"

Sage watched his features tense, and he looked down at the pictures while he spoke. "Well, it's complicated. You know the old South—family and tradition mean everything. My family wasn't happy with me not returning here and going right back to work for the business, but they were patient about it. Then my dad died unexpectedly. Heart attack."

"Oh. I'm sorry. That's awful."

"Yeah. I miss him. He was a great guy—driven but a real family man. He wanted lots of grandchildren, and I hate that he didn't live that long. My sister and I are late bloomers, I guess." He smiled to himself and sighed before continuing. "As the oldest and only boy, I was expected to come right home and fill the gap."

"And you did."

"Yes."

"What do you do?"

"A mix of things, whatever's needed—chair the board, dabble in the legal work. I have implemented an entirely new computer system company-wide. That's been my greatest accomplishment so far."

"Ah. I see."

"What?"

"Hey, birds of a feather—you are as hooked in as I am."

He grinned and nodded. "I guess so. I'd like to do more, but I'm spread rather thin right now. In spite of the situation, I've enjoyed the coding work the last few days."

"Hmm. No other member of your family would be interested in taking your place?"

EJ laughed softly. "Yeah, my sister Grace has been chomping at the bit and resenting me like hell for the last three years. She wanted this position when they called me home, but no one would hear of it."

"Why not?"

"Aw, c'mon—you know that a proper Southern lady is not expected to run a shipping company. Even though she could probably do a better job of it than I'll ever do. She just finished her MBA at Princeton and has always had her fingers in the biz, even though it seems my mother is only interested in seeing her getting an engagement ring on one of them."

"Couldn't you just hand the position over to her? You are the boss, right?"

Sage turned the page, smiling as she realized she had made a suggestion that seemed to startle EJ. He shook his head, laughing.

"Well, you know, I hadn't quite thought of it that way. I suppose you're right, Sage. We'd have to get board approval, but I suppose it's possible."

"Hey—" She furrowed her brow, looking intently down at a photograph, suddenly distracted. "That's Ian." Her voice changed, her eyes glued to the photo. A wedding picture. Her wide eyes met EJ's, questioning. "He's married?"

"Was. A while ago. He's been divorced for some time now. I forgot that was in there. We've known each other a long time."

Sage just studied the photo of Ian standing beside a very attractive young blonde. They looked happy. He was young, maybe early twenties, she guessed. He didn't look as hard as he did now, though he was just as handsome. "What happened?"

"I don't think that's really my place to say. If Ian wants you to know, he should be the one to tell you."

Sage looked back at the picture, her voice soft. "We have a, um, an…"

"An arrangement. I know."

"He told you?"

EJ stood, looking as if he wasn't quite sure what to say. It was the first time she'd ever seen him seem awkward in any way. He stuffed his hands in his pockets and nodded. "It was kind of obvious."

"What do you mean?"

"The way he looks at you—and you at him. The air is electric whenever you two get anywhere near each other."

Sage smirked. "I think you are picking up on how much we tick each other off."

EJ smiled patiently, absently spinning a globe that stood in the corner. "Maybe. Chemistry does weird things to people."

"We don't have chemistry, we just have—"

"An arrangement."

"Yeah."

EJ nodded and looked at her intently. "Well, either way, you can trust him, you know. He's a good man. He'll do his job, he won't let you get hurt. But he's still a man—and he can get hurt, too."

Sage was quiet, letting EJ's caution settle in her mind, when he smiled and sighed.

"Well, I think I'm going to retire for the night. You remember where your room is?"

"Yes. It's lovely. Thank you."

"I'll see you in the morning. Big day tomorrow."

Sage nodded and looked back at the picture of a happier, younger version of Ian staring up at her. Something clicked inside of her, and she closed the book suddenly, putting it back in the pile and shutting off the light. The less she thought about what made Ian happy, the better off she would be. Walking through the dark, she knew it was going to be a long night.

8

IAN OPENED THE FLOOR-TO-ceiling windows in his darkened room and stood staring out into the shadowed greenery of the backyard, thinking through what was about to happen tomorrow from every angle. With any luck at all, they'd have Locke in custody by tomorrow night and all this would be over.

He'd gone to the office to snag a wire for Sage and some other monitoring equipment and now awaited Sarah's arrival in a few hours. EJ would go get her so he and Sage could get some rest. To say Sarah had been willing to help was an understatement—she'd been so excited Ian could hear it in her voice, barely restrained under her usual unshakable cool.

He should be exhausted. Sparing a glance at the bed, he took a deep breath and figured he'd better force himself to get some sleep—though he felt alert now, being tired tomorrow could lead to huge mistakes, and there was no room for error.

The day after next was Sage's release—when Locke implied he would be setting the virus loose. Ian ran a hand through his hair, wondering how things had gotten so crazy so quickly—and wondering what he'd do if this all crashed down around them.

What if Sage was conning them all? What if she really was in cahoots with her ex-lover? His gut twisted at the thought. Just because she appeared to be helping them didn't mean she wasn't simply playing the game well—though the sickened look on her face when he'd mentioned sleeping with Locke had seemed authentic. But that all could be acting.

He was relieved to have Sarah going along with her for several reasons, his lingering suspicions of Sage being part of it. He just hoped he wouldn't be putting Sarah in danger if Sage turned out to be double-crossing them. He supposed he would have to talk with her about that. Or maybe not—it wouldn't do for Sarah to feel less than confident with Sage. No, he would have to keep his doubts to himself, and he and EJ would just have to pay very close attention when the time came.

Ian braced his hands on the wall, letting his head sag forward in exhaustion. None of his decisions felt right, but they felt like the only ones he could make at this point. He'd set the ball rolling in this direction and now he had to see it through. Stepping back toward the wall, he pulled his shirt off and stretched his arms up, trying to get rid of some of the tension straining his body, but it wasn't any use. He wouldn't be able to relax until this was over.

Yanking down the sheets on the bed, he was startled by a knock at the door. Assuming it was EJ, he didn't bother putting his shirt back on and pulled the door open, surprised to find Sage before him in a white robe. Her eyes were smudged with exhaustion, her curls tossed as if she had just rolled out of bed, which was more than likely. The thought caused a warm shimmer to spread throughout his bloodstream. What did she want?

"I thought I heard you moving in here and I, uh, couldn't sleep. I thought we could talk." She answered his unspoken question, and he stood in the doorway, still perplexed by her appearance and fighting the way his body was responding to her being here, now.

"Talk? About what?"

She leveled her gaze with his. "Tomorrow, today—maybe about you."

He felt a sense of apprehension steal over him. "Me?"

She seemed to fumble a bit, sticking her hands inside the pockets of the robe, which caused it to sag a bit at the top, exposing her skin in the dim light of the hallway, and he caught his breath.

"Yeah, um, EJ and I were looking through some pictures earlier and I saw one of you. A wedding picture."

Ian had no idea what to say to that, hoping he appeared more unconcerned than he felt. "So?"

"I didn't know you were married."

"No. Why would you?"

Her eyes burned into his, and she didn't bother keeping her voice down as she responded.

"Oh, well, excuse me. I forget that you've had the right to pry into every—"

"Get in here, jeez, and try keeping it down a little." He pulled her into the room, shutting the door behind. When he turned, he could see she wasn't about to let the matter drop.

"So you get to know every little thing about me, but I'm not expected to know anything about you?"

"You don't need to know anything about me."

His voice was harsh, he knew, and he didn't really mean it to be, but he was caught unawares and he had no idea how to handle this. What did she want from him anyway? And why was she so interested in his past relationships?

"Oh, so in spite of your little lapse into niceness this afternoon, I guess we're back to basics. I'm good enough to bang—"

"Sage…" His voice interrupted her on a warning note, but it didn't stop her.

"But not good enough to talk to? Not deserving enough to know anything about you?"

Her breath was heaving heavily now, and for the second time in a day he saw what he'd never seen in five years—Sage Matthews looking as if she was on the verge of tears. Man, if she was playing with him, she was very good. Walking past her back to the window, where the breeze gently blew the gauzy white curtain into the room, he stood silently for a moment, then turned to face her.

"Fine, okay. I was married. It was a long time ago. Who cares?"

"How long have you been divorced?"

"Almost six years."

"So you were only twenty-seven when you divorced? That's young. When—"

"We got married when we were both twenty-three, fresh out of grad school, right when I started working for the feds. I was recruited at a college job fair, and I thought, hey, let's just do it. Why not? But it didn't work out, and that's pretty much it."

She was staring so intently at him that it was unnerving and he broke away from her gaze. He hadn't talked about this for a very long time, and some of it he had never talked about at all.

"Why?"

The ten-million-dollar question, and the one he really tried to avoid. He told Sage what he told everyone else.

"I was too much into my work, gone a lot, and she didn't want to live that way."

Sage's forehead furrowed. "But you both look so happy in that picture. And it lasted five years, right? She had to know what your job was by then—why would she suddenly object?"

"I guess it just was more than she'd bargained for."

"Did you fool around? Did she?"

Offended, Ian glared at her. "Christ, no. It just… wasn't working. Listen, I really don't want to talk about this."

"Seems like her not liking your job is a pretty flimsy excuse for throwing away a marriage."

Ian swallowed, crossing over to sit on the edge of the

bed. "It's not that easy. I was away a lot, in dangerous situations sometimes. I lived the job and should never have thought I could share my life with a woman, as well. She was great. It was me. I screwed up."

"How?"

If her voice hadn't been so gentle, if she hadn't crossed the room to sit by him, resting her hand on his arm, and if he weren't so tired and feeling as if his life suddenly seemed to be closing in on him, maybe he wouldn't have told her. But as it was, the words tumbled up.

"She—her name was Jen—was pregnant. She told me just shortly before I was assigned a case dealing with a serial rapist who was finding his victims on the Net and attacking them when they arranged a meeting. He'd attacked six women across the country by the time the case landed on my desk."

"I remember that. And I remember he was caught. That was you?"

"Me and my team. We found the next woman he had targeted just as she was making arrangements to meet him. We got involved, tracked the meeting, waited for him to make his move and nabbed him. Went smooth as silk."

Sage's voice was slightly confused. "But that's good, right? What does it have to do with your divorce?"

Ian sighed, stood and walked to the window, hating how the memories triggered emotions that he'd shut away for years.

"Jen called me the day it all went down. She wasn't

feeling well. She'd gone to the doctors, and they were putting her in the hospital for some tests. She was about three months along. I didn't think it was anything critical, so I talked to her on the phone and told her what was happening, that I couldn't get home—remember, the arrest was made in Florida."

Sage just nodded mutely, so he went on.

"Well, it turns out that it was something critical— she'd developed an infection that caused a spontaneous miscarriage that night and might have killed her if she hadn't been in the hospital at the time."

"Oh, God, Ian. That's horrible!"

"I didn't know until the next day, and then it took me another day to get home—I had to be there to get this guy processed."

"And she was alone."

"She had her parents—she wasn't alone in that respect—but she didn't have me. Amazingly she didn't blame me. She wasn't angry. She knew what we'd done was important, saving that woman. But she was heartbroken and depressed afterward, and I guess what really clinched it was that I…I wasn't. I never realized how much the job was taking from me, how little I was giving back to her, to my marriage. I'd been gone so much, was so removed from my life except for work, that I barely was able to grieve when my own baby was lost."

He sighed raggedly. "I couldn't share that pain with her. I felt bad, regretful, but I didn't feel like she did. I guess that was the part she really couldn't forgive me for. And who could blame her?"

Sage was shocked and a little unsure what to say. She hadn't expected this—hadn't expected him to tell her anything, let alone this obviously deeply painful confession.

"I'm sorry, Ian. I'm sorry for all of that. But you were so young still. We all screw up when we're young, and trying to figure things out."

"Thanks, but I made my choices and I live with them. I could have quit, could have chosen to focus on my wife and marriage, but I chose the job, even then. I let her down. She was right to leave." He shook his head, continuing.

"My parents were both career military, they were both gone for long stretches of time, but somehow they made it work. They knew how to balance their sense of duty to their jobs with the duty to each other and their kids. Even when we stayed with other families if they were both gone, we always felt secure. I took that for granted, and really didn't understand how they made it work. I picked up their sense of duty but not the ability to balance it."

"I guess that explains why you are so into following the rules," Sage teased, trying to lighten the moment. A cooler breeze wafted through the windows, causing her to shiver slightly under the thin robe.

"Rules serve a purpose."

"True, and sometimes they need to be bent for better purposes."

"Or broken?"

"Sometimes, yes. People make rules, and since people aren't perfect, neither are rules."

Ian turned, facing her, studying her closely. "That's an interesting perspective but not enough to make it okay to break them when you feel like it. You were raised with rules, just as I was. Maybe not the military, but I know from what I've seen of EJ's family and from what I know of yours that there are some pretty stiff expectations there—and yet you've flouted them all."

"I didn't want anyone telling me how to live my life. I love my family, but they had my whole life planned out for me before I even got a chance to think about what I wanted."

"And what did you want?"

Sage realized he had pretty deftly pivoted the conversation back to being about her, but that was okay. She thought about his question for a few moments.

"I wanted to make my own decisions, mistakes and all. I didn't want to be protected, treated like a little, fragile flower."

"Well, you managed that well enough."

She smiled, as there was soft humor in his response. "Yeah. I managed to get out from under their expectations, but the choices I made were not all that hot either—I went from them being in control of my life to you controlling it."

It was more than she'd ever intended on sharing with him—too honest, too open—but shrouded in the darkness and lateness of the hour, it was a time for telling secrets.

He had opened himself to her, made himself vulnerable—if Ian could ever be thought of as vulnerable. But instead of taking that knowledge and feeling any sense of power, she only felt a need to connect, to share something back.

"Why is control so important to you, Sage? Not that we all don't like some measure of control over our lives, deceptive as it may be, but you seem particularly obsessed with grabbing the reins."

"I guess I just looked at the examples I had in front of me. The women in my family are talented, amazing women. My mom was an artist—or she might have been. I remember tripping across her drawings in her closet once when I was picking through her clothes, playing dress-up."

"And she was good?"

"Oh, they were very good. With training, she might have really done some terrific work. But that wasn't what ladies of her time did—she was engaged by the time she was twenty and pregnant with my sister the year after."

"And she was sad about that?"

Sage thought and then shook her head. "No, she never seemed to be. She liked being a parent, being my dad's wife and serving on museum committees instead of creating art to hang in them."

"So what's so bad?"

"Just that she gave up dreams so easily. And my sister, same deal—she went along like a good little camper, went to college to get a husband instead of an education, quit as soon as she found one, married and has three babies. In spite of the fact that she was at the head of her class in engineering, she just quit to live a *proper* life." Sage wrapped her arms around herself, sighing.

"And you weren't going to let that happen. You weren't going to give up your dreams?"

She was still for a moment, then turned wide eyes to meet his. "That's right, I wasn't. But I guess fate had a good laugh on me, because I ended up losing them anyway, didn't I?"

She looked down, not sure what to do when he was silent. But she felt his hand in her hair, tilting her head back up where he could see her.

"Maybe not lost—just delayed."

"Yeah, right. Like anyone will trust me near a computer now."

"EJ seems to think you have some options. He'll help you."

Sage spoke softly. "What about you?"

He was quiet again, his fingers rubbing against the silk of her hair at the back of her neck. His lips fell to her forehead, his voice low.

"I think you'll find your dreams again, Sage. Just don't let them go, like I did."

She tipped her head back against his hand, gazing up at him. "You didn't let them go, you just chose different ones."

His mouth brushed against hers. It was barely a kiss but had the heat bursting spontaneously between them. Sage hadn't really planned on this happening when she'd decided to knock on his door—maybe she had hoped, somewhere in the corners of her mind, but she hadn't planned it. But as his warm lips worked over hers, she was glad it was happening.

Something was deepening between them, and his touch was different now, more tender, more passionate. She snuggled close and wrapped her arms around his neck, opening to him but demanding back, as well. Landing hot kisses over the skin of her cheek and throat, his voice was hoarse with desire.

"We should be sleeping. Tomorrow…"

Drawing back, she framed his face in her hands and stared into his eyes. "Tomorrow will take care of itself. And we will sleep. After."

Feathering her hands over the smooth, taut skin of his chest, she let her lips follow, suckling, nipping and planting wet kisses wherever she could, losing herself in his taste and his passionate response to her touch.

She sighed with delight when her palm found him hard and rigid under his lightweight pants, and she tugged at his belt.

"Time for these to go." She smiled wickedly, yanking the leather from the loop, looking up in surprise when his hand stopped her.

"Sage, as much as I want to, I, um, we don't have anything here. Protection."

Sage bit her lip. Her body was humming with need

for him, and there was no way she was going back to bed without satisfying that need. She tugged the belt through the remaining loops, her voice loaded with suggestion.

"I guess we'll just have to be creative then, won't we?"

He moaned and released her as she delved into his naval with her tongue, simultaneously loosening the zipper of his slacks. He helped her shuck them quickly, and she stood by the side of the bed with him looking at her hungrily.

Slowly she unwrapped the robe and let it drop from her shoulders, his sharp intake of breath and the jerk of his erection egging her on. Smiling, she hooked a thumb through her thong—the only thing she had on—and rather than pulling them down, slid her hand underneath, reaching down between her thighs, finding her own hot, moist center.

"Sage…" Ian's voice was full of delighted surprise, and she stroked herself lightly, shuddering with the pleasure of it, and it was ten times more pleasurable with him watching. But that was only the beginning— apparently he had a few surprises for her, as well. Watching him reach down and wrap his hand around himself, she gasped, equally delighted and turned on when he stroked as he watched her. After a few moments, his breath coming hard, he reached his other hand out to her.

"Come here."

"Just a sec." Her knees were weak as heat throbbed

through her, but she also felt ecstatically in control. She turned her back to him, hooked her fingers into the thin scrap of material she was wearing and proceeded to slip it downward, bending slightly so that he had the most erotic vantage point she could manage. His deep, masculine groan washed over her, and she turned, smiling seductively.

"Watch out, Ian. Here I come."

IAN WASN'T COMPLETELY sure what to expect, but he was pretty much open to anything that included Sage naked on the bed. She walked toward him, her gait slow and sensual, and he reached down to stroke himself once more, watching her eyes follow his movements, her sexy voice urging him on.

"That's it, Ian. Let me watch you."

She slid up next to him, kneeling beside him on the firm mattress, sliding her hands up to her breasts while she watched, small whimpers and sighs becoming all she could utter as she saw his body, aroused and hard. The cool breeze from the window washed over her, caressing her everywhere, brushing across her stiff nipples as she reached down, seeking her own release. Ian's hand reached out, stopping her, and she looked down, questions in her eyes.

"Come here."

This time she obeyed the command quickly, scuttling up next to him where he had pushed himself back to rest against the headboard. He turned to his side, and she followed suit. Wordlessly he took her mouth in a long, drugging kiss, his hands finding her breasts, massaging and pinching until she almost came with no further help at all.

"Ian...I need..."

He laughed softly against her mouth. "Me, too." His hands left her breasts to guide her hand to his cock, closing over hers, showing her what he liked. Sage cried out when he slipped his other hand deftly between her thighs, finding her sweet spot immediately, stroking her into an almost instant orgasm. She bucked under his hand, losing track of exactly what she was doing to him, though she never stopped her own movements.

He was groaning, nudging his head into the soft space between her neck and shoulder, saying her name and pushing against her insistently. She felt him get impossibly hard and hot in her palm. He was close, and as she felt him start to quiver, he slid one finger, then two, inside her, thrusting deep, stroking in such a way as pleasure built.

Hooking a leg over his, she wound them together, locking them tightly and giving him better access. He erupted in her hand at the very moment she felt the pressure building inside her release itself, a sweet, hot pulse that shook her from head to toe.

Catching her breath, she continued massaging him, letting her head fall back against the soft pillow, her hair plastered against her damp forehead. He fluttered his fingers over her most sensitive areas, causing her to shudder once more, then he pulled her close.

She stayed in his arms for a moment. Then, feeling the swamping emotions that came along with such intimate contact, she disentangled herself, inching over a bit to the other side of the bed. Her skin was still hot, but she shivered, and he glanced at her curiously, rising to close the window before returning to the bed. Lying back down, he rolled on his side and faced her, raising a hand to push some hair back from her face, his eyes narrowing when she flinched a bit.

"Sage, what's wrong?"

"Nothing's wrong. That was great. It was…great."

"Then why are you pulling away?"

She slid from the bed to grab the robe on the floor, tying it around her. Feeling overly exposed and confused, she spoke, hating that her voice was quavering.

"Listen, this is just sex, right? In another day or so we'll finish this and go our separate ways."

Ian waited a beat, then said. "I guess that's right."

She sighed, feeling a stab even though she'd expected him to agree.

"Right. So we had great sex. When you are so… when you hold me like that, it confuses me. I don't like it," she lied, her traitorous heart whispering exactly how much she liked it. Needed it, even.

Ian lay still, not bothering to cover himself or dress, regarding her silently.

"I do that for me as much as for you—it may be just sex, Sage, but that doesn't mean we can't be nice to each other. It doesn't have to be harsh or unfeeling because it's just sex."

Her heart was pounding in her ears. If he said "just sex" one more time, she was going to scream. Because, as sure as the sun was going to rise very shortly, it was becoming more than just sex for her.

"I'm going to go back to my own room."

"Okay."

Turning before she made a bigger fool of herself, she walked out with as much dignity as she could muster, hoping she looked somewhat casual, though she felt nothing of the sort. Her plan to seduce Ian and keep control of the game was backfiring—her emotions were betraying her.

He'd been so good to her earlier in the day, then had shared some of the deepest moments of his past with her and had held her so gently—it was all messing with her heart, and that messed with her head, as well.

Entering her room, she closed the door quietly behind her and went over to the large mahogany bed. A cool breeze fluttered the curtains away from the window, and she frowned—she hadn't opened any windows. Or maybe she had and forgotten. She didn't think any more about it and crawled in between the sheets, trying to ignore how lonely she felt curling up by herself.

As she placed her head on the pillow, she heard a crackling sound, her cheek laying down on what felt like paper. Lifting her head up, she discovered a piece of notepaper. She froze, looking to the window and holding the note in her hand for several moments before swinging her legs over the side of the bed, her heart hammering. The paper was the same as the first note from Locke. He'd been here. She opened it with shaking fingers.

LadyBug,
In case you haven't been able to figure out the clues I left you, I decided to drop by for a visit. Does it surprise you that I have been watching? I have seen...everything. Sleeping with the enemy, my love? As disturbing as I find it, I can only assume you are doing what must be done to distract and control him. But don't enjoy it too much and think of me. We'll be together soon.
Locke

Sage finally gave in to the tears that had been threatening at every turn all day. Lying back on the bed, the note falling to the floor, she met the dawn by letting herself have a good, long cry.

9

IAN WAS SEATED AT THE table with a stunning brunette when Sage walked in the next morning, and she was taken aback for a second before realizing this had to be Sarah. God, she looked like a movie star—one of those kick-ass action-adventure stars that could fight off seven guys and not have a hair out of place. Her calm blue eyes met Sage's, and she smiled slightly before turning her attention back to Ian, who was filling her in.

Sage ran a hand through her disheveled curls—they were impossible in the humidity, and she wished for Sarah's sleek look. Sage knew she definitely did not look like a movie star. EJ was fussing with something at the stove, and the kitchen was filled with wonderful smells that had lured her out of the deep sleep she'd fallen into after soaking in a nice, long, self-indulgent cry. She'd felt all the better for it until she'd remembered the note and brought it downstairs. This was really going to make everyone's morning.

EJ turned, smiling. "Morning, Sage. Grab some coffee and we'll eat. Need a substantial breakfast when you are planning to catch a bad guy."

Sage moved into the kitchen and then Sarah stood, and Sage's eyebrows raised in disbelief—God, she was tall, too. Before she could react, Sarah stuck her hand out in Sage's direction.

"Hi. I'm Sarah. It sounds like we'll be working together."

Sage looked at Ian and then up at Sarah. She placed her hand in Sarah's and returned her firm grip. The two women regarded each other speculatively for a second, and Sage spoke as their hands released. "That's what I hear. You must have just gotten in?"

"About an hour ago."

Sage sat down and held on to a large cup of coffee, resenting how the woman could not only look great but be a bundle of energy after she'd obviously been up all night. Sarah had so much energy it practically reverberated around the kitchen.

Sage reached for the note in her pocket as EJ plopped a large platter of eggs and crab cakes down on the table, followed by a bowl filled with chunks of spicy corn bread. Sage smiled up at him.

"Millie's right—she's going to have a heck of a time staying thin with how you cook."

He laughed and grabbed a piece of corn bread. "Just means there'll be more to love." Sage watched his gaze switch from her to Sarah, who was happily devouring everything he put in front of her.

"Can I get you anything else? You must be exhausted. And starved."

Sarah just grinned and shook her head. "No, I'm fine, this is great."

Sage finally got up the nerve to tell everyone about the note and jumped into the conversation.

"There's something you all need to know. Something happened last night."

She thought she saw a flicker of panic on Ian's face before he spotted the paper she slid onto the table.

"What's that?"

Sage pushed the note toward him. He opened it and swore as he threw it back down on the table, his face dark and angry.

"Dammit. He was here in the house."

"Who?" EJ sat and took a sip of coffee, almost choking when Ian spoke again.

"Locke. He was in Sage's room last night. He left this note."

EJ put his hand on her arm. "Jesus, are you okay? I know I set the alarm before I went to bed."

Sage felt heat rush up into her face. "No doubt he disarmed it. I, um, wasn't there when he came in."

EJ read the note and passed it to Sarah, discreetly not asking where Sage had been. Sarah read the note, her brow wrinkling.

"So what does he mean you're sleeping with the enemy? Isn't he the enemy?"

She looked up at the three awkward expressions on the faces of the people seated around the table and arched one cool eyebrow, her gaze drifting between

Ian and Sage, her mouth forming into a silent "Oh." Putting the note down, she took a hearty bite of crab cake.

"Sounds like he assumes you're, uh, doing it for, you know, good reasons. Still, pretty creepy." Looking down, she continued eating.

Sage knew Locke must have seen her and Ian together, probably on the balcony, she realized with regret as she remembered the boats floating peacefully out on water. Now he was really going to expect her to prove her loyalty.

"He's obviously been watching us very closely."

"I should go to meet him alone. He's never going to go for someone else being there. He'll figure Sarah for another fed."

"You are not going alone." Ian's voice brooked no argument, but Sage started to give him one anyway, until EJ broke in thoughtfully. "He may not have seen me come home with Sarah—he may have just broken into your room and left."

"What if he thinks you've switched teams?"

Everyone looked at Sarah, perplexed. She sat back, looking at them all in amusement. "You know, as in not part of the heterosexual camp anymore? Would he be likely to leave you alone then?"

Sage shook her head. "He knows about me and Ian."

"Sure, but you could say you were just doing what you had to do to protect yourself."

Sage thought that over for a moment. "He might go for that. Maybe we could still play the girlfriend angle and take the position that if you don't get to play, I won't either."

"The important thing is stalling him the best you can and getting to that source computer. EJ and I will wire Sarah, as he is less likely to put his hands on her." Ian's eye's became shuttered as he spoke the thought aloud, but he continued on. "And we'll be close by. No more than a minute away if things go sour. I've already talked with Marty and we'll have backup if we need it. Fast."

"Who's Marty?" Sarah inquired and Ian smiled a little.

"The guy you scared the crap out of in my office the day you came in to interview. He's my boss—and yours by extension, by the way."

Sarah looked at Ian, her eyes not giving too much away, but Ian could sense the questions bubbling underneath the surface. "My boss? I thought this was just a freelance gig."

"Think of it more as a trial run. EJ might be the other member of the team and this is a chance to find out how we'll all work together."

EJ piped in, offering the last piece of corn bread around the table before claiming it for himself. "Heck of a risky experiment, Ian. There's a lot on the line."

Ian nodded. "It's under control. If everyone just plays their part, we'll have this guy behind bars while we eat breakfast tomorrow. As stings go, this is pretty straightforward. Believe me, it can get much messier."

Sage looked up, uncertainty written plainly on her

features. "What if doesn't work? Tomorrow is my release date. What happens if we don't catch him?"

Ian didn't meet her eyes when he answered. "I guess we'll just have to take that as it comes." He pushed away from the table. "For now, I think we need to go over the plan a few more times, and you and Sarah need to get to know each other a little better if you are going to pull this off. Locke may be a dirtbag, but he's definitely not stupid."

AFTER BREAKFAST IAN SAT alone in EJ's office, staring at a file that Marty had sent over to him. Sarah's background check. She hadn't finished college, which he'd known, but now he knew why, and his reactions ranged from shock to disgust. She'd been put through the wringer, that's for sure, and it was no longer a mystery why she devoted the majority of her time to busting Internet porn rings.

Apparently one of her boyfriends had gotten the bright idea to set up secret cameras in his dorm room—the girls he'd brought back there chosen particularly for their potential appeal as candidates for the porn Web site he ran off the campus servers. How it had gone undetected for so long—two years—was dumbfounding. But the damage that had been done when the site was busted and pictures of several female students—including Sarah—had gotten released on the Net was considerable.

Some of those pictures were included in the file, as well as newspaper articles and television coverage. It was no surprise that Sarah had left the school shortly after, even though she had been a star student before that event. Ian guessed it was impossible for her to have a normal life there after the pictures and the site had become public knowledge.

He dropped the file on the desk and wasn't sure how to handle this new information. He sympathized, but he also needed to make clear, objective decisions about who he put on the team.

Looking at his watch, he saw he'd been in the office for almost two hours. It was getting close to time for them to start preparing to meet Locke—the clues had suggested he'd be there in the early evening, when he and Sage had apparently met there many times before. Eight would be the magic hour. Ian was grateful it stayed light even past nine this time of year.

Knowing that and knowing the creep wanted her back in his bed again made Ian's blood boil. He was glad Sarah was going along—her untried, untrained investigative skills would be a plus this time around. She wasn't a cop—yet—and so she wouldn't be giving off cop vibes. She'd be an easier sell.

Then again, considering her past, could she go in there and act as though she wanted to go to bed with this guy, a virtual stranger? Would she crack under the pressure? Ian wasn't sure, but he didn't want Sage left alone with Locke, and Sarah was on board now. A knock at the door made him jump, and he turned. EJ walked in.

"How's it going? I think the ladies have their game

on, so we're ready to get started." EJ walked up to the desk, noting the concern in Ian's expression. "Something wrong?"

Ian barked out a humorless laugh. "Just about everything. But that aside, well, I'm less than sure about sending Sarah in with Sage. I know she has computer skills, but I hope I'm making the right call sending her in on something like this."

"She seems to be tough, smart. Clearly a woman who can handle herself and most anyone else she comes across."

"True. And I guess it's too late for second-guessing now. We'll just have to be sharp—if anything seems like it's going down wrong, we're in there."

"I'm ready."

Ian eyed his friend, noting the energy that zinged through his usual calm demeanor, the spark in his eye, and smiled. He had no doubt EJ would find a way to join the team—he loved this stuff.

"Good."

"Sarah's background file?" EJ nodded to the file on the desk and grinned. "Gonna have me worked up, as well?"

"You I know about. But, yeah, for purposes of keeping the process equal, I'll be checking out all your dirty little secrets, as well."

"Happy reading."

"Where's Millie tonight?"

EJ visibly tensed. "She's staying at her sister's. I sort of mentioned something was going on, and she doesn't like it, so she did what she usually does—avoids anything that disrupts the way she wants life to be."

"Nice if you can do it."

"Some folks can afford to."

"I take it she's not a huge supporter of your return to law enforcement then?"

"Haven't brought it up to her. Just said I was helping you out."

"She likes me, but she never did approve of me—I've been a bad influence on you." Ian laughed but sobered when EJ didn't. EJ fell into a deep chair across from Ian, elbows planted on his knees, and dropped his head into his hands, obviously struggling with some serious decisions.

"Yeah, when this is over, I think…shit."

"What?" Ian knew what was next but let the conversation spin out on its own.

"I just think…I don't know, maybe we should call it off. I haven't told her about the HotWires thing, but I know she will side with my family when I tell them I'm quitting."

Ian perked up. "You are?"

EJ nodded. "As soon as I figure out how. But Millie has her heart set on a certain kind of life, and I've never been sure it's the life I want. And we just don't have as much…heat between us as we used to. She's a wonderful friend, and when we were young I thought she was it for me, but… Hell. I don't know."

"Things change. If the magic's not there, EJ, you're doing her as much a favor as you're doing yourself cutting it off before you have bigger problems and a ring on your finger, a couple of kids in tow."

EJ nodded, looking up, quirking a tense smile. "Ha. You're biased. You want me in this job."

"I want you happy. I think we've been friends the longest of anyone I've known since we moved here. Millie's great, but, well, you know. I just always wondered if you were in it with her because you wanted to be or because you were expected to be."

EJ exhaled heavily, his eyes resigned. "You're a very perceptive man. It's going to hurt her, though."

Ian stood, slapping him on the shoulder supportively. "You'll find a way. Life's too short, Ethan. You've done right by everyone for a long time. It's time for you to start following your own path."

EJ sighed. "Things have suddenly gotten very complicated."

"That's what makes life interesting, huh?"

EJ laughed, as well, standing. "Yeah, something like that. So let's get the show on the road."

SAGE SET HER JAW AND assumed a gunslinger stance, gearing up for her next "rehearsal" with Sarah, who collapsed in laughter as she watched Sage's antics.

"Hey, that's not fair. We're supposed to be being sexy."

"You don't find cowboys sexy?"

Sarah groaned and made a "bring it on" gesture with her hands. "C'mon, show me how sexy you are, *girlfriend.*"

They were having a great time. Though it had been awkward at first—they were strangers trying to act like they were more than friends—Sarah's no-nonsense, get-things-done demeanor had taken over, and soon they were brainstorming and role-playing so that they could appear "very close" in front of Locke.

Sage was having fun and felt more at ease with Sarah than she did even with her own sister. Sarah was just a little bit older than she was, closer to thirty, but she was cool. They joked and chatted in between the role-playing, and soon they were having fun hamming it up as a lesbian version of Thelma and Louise.

They heard the library door close and Ian's and EJ's voices in the hall. Sarah's eyes suddenly sparkled with mischief, and she darted a look toward the hall, then back at Sage.

"Wanna mess with the guys?"

"Always."

"Wanna really shock 'em?"

Sage smiled, knowing what Sarah had in mind, but she felt apprehensive. While she felt comfortable with Sarah, she felt uncomfortable on many levels with this entire situation. Still, they would have to pull this off in front of Locke, so they might as well practice in front of Ian and EJ to see if they were convincing at all. The two women eyed each other with steely purpose in their gazes.

"I'm game if you are."

"Bring it on, sista."

IAN AND EJ HEARD ONLY some muffled conversation as they approached the main room, then stopped short in the doorway, their conversation completely cut off as they watched Sage and Sarah "practice." Ian didn't know what he had expected, but it wasn't *this*.

The two women were plastered up against each other, their mouths meeting in fluttering little butterfly kisses until Sarah yanked Sage forward and glued her lips onto the other woman's. Sage petted Sarah's long hair and pressed herself even closer, seemingly oblivious to the men's presence.

Ian wanted to clear his throat, wanted to say something, but his voice had deserted him. He was completely aware they were just practicing so they could be natural in front of Locke, but he was finding himself— a little surprisingly—getting turned on. He had gay friends and he'd seen them kiss, hold hands and whatnot and never thought anything of it. But the sight of these two beautiful women kissing was definitely striking up the band. Damn.

As the kiss lingered and Sage and Sarah gazed sexily at each other, he started wondering if there were some things about Sage he didn't know after all. Maybe he even felt a little jealous. She looked so…into it. So did Sarah, for that matter. He knew they were supposed to be believable, but it still rattled him, and he had an enormous urge to pull Sage away.

Not knowing what exactly to make of the situation, he looked to EJ, only to find his friend also staring at the women. Just as Ian was about to hit the panic button, the women burst apart in a gale of laughter, holding their sides in hysterics.

He and EJ stood still in the doorway as the women took turns doing dramatic bows to each other and to them. A wave of desire passed over him as Sage rose from her bow, her sparkling eyes and flushed cheeks showing a playful side of her he hadn't seen. She looked like a kid having the time of her life. Her impish gaze met his, and she grinned even more broadly, bowing again.

He was unprepared for the emotions that rose from his chest into his throat, settling in a lump there, as he realized how truly beautiful she was. He'd always been attracted to her, but when she sparkled like that she was dazzling.

He could only guess how much more stunning she would be if she were really, truly happy. It opened her up, brightened her like sunshine. What if all the walls, defenses and tough attitudes were abandoned and she let him see her true self? Suddenly he found himself wanting nothing more, and it scared the crap out of him.

"So were we convincing?" Sarah's voice, breathless with laughter, cut through the haze Ian found himself in. EJ answered before he could.

"Oh, yeah."

Sarah raised her eyebrows at EJ's admiring tone and grinned widely, bobbing her head and high-fiving Sage.

"Cool. We're hot, sista. The boys can barely breathe."

"You'll have him hook, line and sinker."

The atmosphere in the room suddenly became serious again as Ian's comment reminded them of what lay ahead. They all sat down at the table and started going over their plan one more time.

10

LOCKE ALWAYS LOVED THIS spot, and thank God it hadn't changed over the years. Too much was changing and he didn't like it. Settling back into an old wooden chair at one of the tiny tables that lined the walls of the bar, he placed a ginger ale on the table, peering at the early-evening crowd. Ginger ale was good because it looked like something alcoholic but wasn't—he needed to blend in to the bar atmosphere, but he liked keeping sharp.

The usual mix of college students and yuppie couples were all huddled over drinks, books or each other. No one paid attention to anyone else in the small, dim atmosphere of the place. He'd chosen a corner table— it was dark, private and even kind of romantic. After all, part of his goal here was to get his lady back.

It had been disappointing and aggravating to find LadyBug's room empty the night before—he'd finally had enough of watching her with the cop and his frustration had gotten the better of him. He hadn't wanted to wait. But when he'd found her room empty, he'd known he'd been granted a reprieve—it would have blown everything for him to go to her. She had to come to him.

He wanted her in his bed, yes. And when he had her there, she would forget all about the cop. But he wanted more than that. He wanted her back. Back with him, back in the game. Back to their side of the cause. And he'd figured out just how to keep her with him forever.

SAGE SAT QUIETLY NEXT to Ian in the car as they drove to the bar. Sarah and EJ were sitting in the backseat, talking, but she didn't hear a word they were saying, didn't see anything that was moving past her on the other side of the window as the car sped along. Her hands were numb with nerves and she couldn't seem to unclench them.

She wondered what it would be like to have a normal life. A stable, happy life. An image from a magazine she'd been paging through before they'd left—an old white farmhouse with flowers everywhere and children playing in the yard—had called to someplace deep inside of her, and she'd had another one of those unexpected wellings of emotion.

It reminded her of being a kid, how life was before things got complicated. She'd had a good childhood—it was the last time she could remember being happy. How had that life become so unbearable?

Questions she'd never considered, things she'd never thought of, were hitting her lately. She loved her family, but at some point she'd felt so smothered by them, she'd just railed against everything. The consequences had been harsh.

Now things just seemed to be bubbling up within her after being capped for years, and she hated it. But it also made her think about what she wanted from the life that would be at her fingertips if everything went well and her freedom was granted her. Maybe a nice white farmhouse someday? Some kids? She rolled her eyes at the thought. Maybe, as Ray had said, normal wasn't meant for her.

Still, she wondered what it would be like. Could you have all that and not lose who you were? She went over her conversation with Ian last night. He'd asked her why she'd done the things she'd done. Had her mother and sister really lost their identities or just forged new ones? What was she so afraid of?

She had rebelled against everything "normal" when she was growing up, for reasons she couldn't even begin to understand, but she was getting tired. Tired of fighting all the time, tired of not knowing what the next day was going to be like, what the rest of her life was going to be like. A little stability might be nice, after all.

She glanced covertly at Ian, who stared straight out at the road. He hadn't had a normal life either, though certainly a more stable one. One structured by clear rules and definitions of right and wrong. Instead of flouting the rules, he had embraced them, made them part of who he was. In that way, they couldn't be more different.

There was a certain level of security in the rules, she guessed. She had never had to worry about where her next meal was coming from or anything like that, but she felt adrift. Unsettled, unsure and, if she was completely honest, unhappy.

Her life had been so structured for the last five years and so determined by others up to this point—her parents, Locke, the courts—what was to come next? When she was younger she'd thought that was an exciting question, but more and more it was a lonely one. A depressing one. Her future appeared before her as an indefinable blur.

Sage wrapped her arms around herself, shivering as the AC blasted out from the vents. She suspected the answer was somewhere in the middle—Ian had a hard time breaking the rules and she had a hard time following them. They were at extremes, both butting heads in the middle.

But at the moment she thought it might not be so bad to have a few rules to hang on to, a few things in life you could count on. Of course, if this thing with Locke blew up in her face, she wouldn't have to worry about it. The fine state of Virginia would make sure she had all the stability and rules she needed for a very long time.

"Worried?" Ian's voice broke into her reverie.

"No," she lied.

"Great. We won't be far away, and you'll have Sarah. This is going to go down fine. Remember, all you need to do is get him to agree to take you to his place. If he even so much as gives you the address, that's all we need."

Sage nodded as they pulled up a few streets over from the Blue Shark. She and Sarah would pick up a car they had dropped there earlier and drive to the other street, where the bar was located, just in case Locke was on the lookout. Walking was not an option—he would know they'd been dropped. As Sage reached for the handle to open the car door, she found her hand trapped by Ian's, his long fingers squeezing hers.

"Stick with the plan, Sage. Don't improvise. And we'll be right here," he said, his voice steady and confident.

Sage just nodded, her heart in her throat, as she and Sarah got out of the car. The game was on, and her future was the prize.

"WHOA. THAT'S HIM?" Sarah whispered in Sage's ear as they peered through the small window in the door before entering. Sage spotted Locke immediately and her skin turned clammy.

"Yeah. That's him."

"I've heard about his exploits for years. And that's the man himself." Sage looked at her, one brow raised at Sarah's awed tone.

Sarah smiled self-consciously. "Sorry, he's sort of a celebrity, even if he is a jerk. Little does he know he's heading for prison."

Sage smirked, studying Locke through the glass for

a few moments more. He was wearing black, as always, and had a light beard now.

"Hey, you going in or are you just gonna peep through the window all night?" A rude voice inquired from behind, and she glared at a bunch of frat boys obviously waiting to gain entrance to the bar. When Sarah and Sage turned around, the guys' faces lit up in appreciation of finding two good-looking women facing them, and the one who'd spoken leered openly, his voice going from rude to ruder.

"Come to think of it, you can peep in my windows anytime."

Sage saw Sarah's blue eyes darken dangerously. When she spoke, her voice was soft but cutting.

"Yeah, well, that's tempting but to see *anything* I imagine we'd have to look very, *very* closely."

The ringleader's face turned crimson as his pals slapped him and laughed at the burn, and he started to respond. Sarah stepped forward, ready to mix it up, but Sage pulled her back toward the door.

"We don't have time for this. C'mon."

Sarah gave the guys one last dirty look and stepped inside.

"I hate guys like that. Treat women like pieces of meat. Sorry."

"It's okay, no harm done."

Sage went over to the bar to order drinks for her and Sarah. She took a sip of a nonalcoholic amaretto sour, then as she turned her head, her eyes immediately met Locke's dark ones.

She had thought him handsome at one point, but now he just looked…cruel. Hard. Scary. Ignoring the slamming of her pulse, she smiled at Sarah and beckoned her to follow.

As they approached the table and Locke saw she wasn't alone, his smile faded.

"Who's this? You were supposed to come alone."

Sage pouted and took another sip of her drink. "That's a hell of a way to say hello after so long, Locke. And I'm taking a huge risk sneaking out to see you. Sarah helped me, so you should be grateful. But we need to make this quick—if they find I got out, this is over for all of us."

His gaze was suspicious. "I said, who is this?"

Sarah slid down into the chair opposite Locke's. "I'm Sarah Jessup. I'm a friend of LadyBug's and a big…fan of yours."

Locke's gaze traveled from Sarah to Sage, and finally Sage sighed dramatically and shot him the sexiest smile she could muster, sliding her hand over Sarah's shoulder and slipping her forefinger under the thin spaghetti strap of her top.

"I'm sorry, Locke, but I wasn't sure what to expect when I saw you and I just felt more…secure with Sarah along."

A glint of sick satisfaction showed in his expression when she admitted to being afraid of him, the bastard. She should have known that would appeal to him, though he continued to inquire.

"Why would that be exactly?"

Sage tilted her head to gaze seductively at Sarah, covering Sarah's hand with her own. "We're…close. Sarah is my moral support. Has been for a long time. I figured you'd know that—if you've been watching me."

Locke's eyes landed on their clasped hands and his eyebrows arched.

"I've been out of the country. I haven't been watching for five years, baby girl, I'm a busy man. Besides, I knew where you were. Your situation wasn't likely to change." He laughed harshly. "You expect me to believe you two are together? I've seen you with the cop—screwing his eyes out of his sockets. Does your *girlfriend* know about that? Or is she a cop, too?"

Sarah burst out laughing and Sage just smiled and shushed her, as if they shared in the joke. Locke apparently didn't think it was so funny.

"Be nice, please, Locke? She's a hacker, just like me. We're careful because seeing her could get me thrown back in jail. She's also the only…friend I've had in a long time. You deserted me, after all, and what's a girl to do?"

Sage held her breath, but she could see him processing what she said.

"And the cop?"

Sage waved her hand. "Yeah, that sucked. Sorry about that, but I did what I had to do after he got suspicious. God knows I didn't enjoy it. You weren't exactly subtle about dropping the disk—it put me in a tough spot."

Sarah played her part and cooed at Sage comfortingly.

"So you aren't into men anymore? That could present a problem."

Sage smiled. "I'm not into *cops*. But screwing him served a purpose—an insurance policy, so to speak. This way he won't give me any trouble. He knows about you, but he doesn't really care as long as I keep him happy. See what I've been willing to do for you?"

She moved away from Sarah and slithered onto Locke's lap, hooking her arm around his shoulder. "So you see, I am into Sarah. We're into each other. But I'm into you, too. We both are. We couldn't wait to see you. I was so disappointed when you were gone last night."

Sage kept her cool, staring into his eyes with what she hoped was a persuasive degree of desire considering she wanted to vomit when she felt him harden beneath her thigh.

"I don't like thinking of you with other men."

She reached up to stroke his hair. "I haven't really been with any other men. Like I said, the cop was a necessity. But after you, I just couldn't find anyone as…satisfying. And Sarah, well—" she turned her head and smiled suggestively at Sarah "—is obviously not a man."

That seemed to make Locke more relaxed. "I see that. You have good taste, LadyBug. I'll give you that."

Sarah tipped her drink back, finishing it. "So now that we're all friends, where's the party?"

Locke raised an inquiring eyebrow while stroking

Sage's bare back—the summer dress she'd worn didn't leave much to the imagination—and Sarah sighed impatiently.

"Sage, I don't like being left over here by myself. You two look pretty cozy, but what about me?"

Locke laughed and nuzzled Sage's cheek while his fingers traced lightly over her hip. "You don't like to watch? You might have to get used to it, baby."

Sage watched something unpleasant snap to life in Sarah's eyes, a quick flicker of disgust that Locke would probably put down to jealousy. Sarah leaned forward, staring him in the eye, her gaze full of sensual promises, her tone sultry.

"I'd rather play." She looked at Sage with full-on lust in her eyes. "Or you could watch us. Fine by me."

Locke looked a little surprised, but he was definitely interested. Sage knew this because the heat from his body was intense and the lazy circles he drew on her back became even more suggestive, dipping lower. She wasn't going to be able to sit there so intimately pressed up against him for much longer. Seeing an escape route, she took it, returning to Sarah.

Pulling a chair up close, she faced Sarah, stroking her hair and leaning in to kiss her cheek. "Don't worry, honey, we aren't going to leave you behind. I told you this would all work out."

Sage met Locke's gaze and realized he was buying it—he was getting totally turned on watching them together. Apparently EJ and Ian were right about this scenario fueling men's fantasies.

"So we're cool, Locke?"

"I'm sure we can work something out. I'd looked forward to…having you for myself, LadyBug, but three can definitely be company."

Sarah smiled at him and Sage sat back, the flirtation evaporating from her expression as she cut to the chase. They had him where they wanted him now, and she intended to keep him there.

"But let's talk business before pleasure."

Locke's hard smile was sharp even in the dingy light, and Sage felt herself shiver when he reached across the table to drag the back of his fingers down the curve of her cheek, pulling the tip of his thumb over her lip.

"You always did know what I liked, LadyBug."

"Not always. I thought you liked *me*." Sage hoped she was injecting the right amount of hurt into her voice.

"What's that supposed to mean?"

"You hung me out to dry, Locke. Taking the fall and being left to deal with it by myself. Do you have any idea what the last five years have been like? What the rest of my life is going to be like? How can I ever live a normal life again? You, you can do anything you want, but I have a record now. I was lucky not to end up in prison." Sage's voice hissed out, and Locke pursed his lips, looking unimpressed.

"We all have to make sacrifices, baby girl. You made yours. But don't worry, I'll do right by you. The past is over, and you don't have to worry about the future. You've proved yourself."

"Oh, really? Ever try to get a job with a felony record?"

Locke laughed and shook his head. "Poor, sweet thing. You never did see the larger picture. Jobs are for drones. You're better than that."

"Nice words, Locke, but what do they mean?"

"It means I'll take care of you, baby girl, but you have to take care of me, too. You and your friend."

"How? Did you get rich when I wasn't looking?"

"Don't worry about that. Let's just say launching this bug will be the final step in showing me that you are on my side."

Sage blinked. "You say that like you expect me to do it."

Locke smiled, sliding a zip disk across the table. "That's exactly right."

IAN LISTENED QUIETLY on one set of headphones while EJ sat stoically listening on the other. Ian's nimble fingers played over the laptop, typing in any leads he tried to pick up from Sage's discussion with Locke. At least they were in a good spot in the bar—there wasn't too much background noise, and their voices were coming through clear.

Ian didn't allow himself to think of anything else. He just monitored, disciplined in his role as a cool observer. In his job, he often had to sit back and watch, wait, difficult as it often was. But it was usually worth it once the moment came to strike.

He didn't think about Sage sitting there with Locke,

how he was probably looking at her or touching her. No, he wouldn't think about that.

"Good girl. Get him to talk about that code," Ian whispered, hearing Sage turn the conversation to the disk and the virus. Then he and EJ looked at each other as the conversation took a new turn—she was going off on him about setting her up. That wasn't in the plan.

"What the hell? Aw, c'mon, Sage, don't improvise now. Dammit. She's gonna piss him off."

Ian banged his head back against the headrest, and EJ placed a hand on his shoulder, looking at him soberly.

"She's doing it for you. She wants you to know she was telling the truth about being set up."

Ian blinked. Shit. What was worse was realizing he hadn't really believed her, not completely, and he felt guilty as hell. She was taking chances to prove something to him. If this went sideways, it would be as much his fault as hers. Rubbing a hand across his face, he nodded to EJ. "Yeah, and it could screw the entire thing up if this guy gets pissed and leaves."

"Oh, crap," EJ whispered to himself as he continued listening to what was being said in the bar.

They heard Locke's plan—he wanted Sage to be his fall guy again. Did he really think she'd be that gullible, that stupid? But maybe this was the magic carpet ride they needed to wherever he was hiding his computer.

The voices were muffled through the headphones, a little fuzzier now as the bar became more crowded and the background noise louder. Ian hit some commands to try to block it out. He heard Sage ask incredulously if Locke wanted her to be the one to let the virus free again and his chilling answer.

"That's exactly right."

Sage's laugh came across so loud and sharp—she must be close to Sarah and the bug—that Ian jumped. Her voice communicated clearly what she thought of that plan.

"Yeah, right. Fool me once…"

"No fooling around this time, Sage. Here." Ian heard a shuffling and assumed Locke was handing Sage something. "You take this and hit the hot button. When I can see it's been executed, I'll tell you where to meet me and we'll go. No cops, no one will find us or even know until it's much too late. We'll be gone, living the good life."

"I'm supposed to believe that? How is this supposed to happen exactly? That we will all be living the good life?"

"That's for me to know. You just trust me, baby girl."

Ian heard the cynicism in Sage's voice and knew there was no acting going on now.

"Trust you? You cost me five years of my life! And you want me to trust you? No way, I'm out. Forget it. Sarah, we're outta here."

Ian heard the chairs shuffle and panicked for a moment—was she really going to walk away? Did she at least grab the disk? Then he heard Locke calling her name, laughing. He really was a cocky bastard. There was a bit more of a scuffle and Sage's voice clearly saying "Ow!" Ian's hand was on the car door handle before he could take another breath, but EJ caught him by the shoulder and shook his head, holding up one finger, signaling him to wait.

"LadyBug, it's nice to see you aren't as easy as you were before. I like a challenge. But don't think you can ever just get up and walk out on me. Now sit back down and we're going to talk."

There was a moment of silence and Ian held his breath, then he heard her respond.

"Fine." Her voice had a slight wince in it, and Ian felt his blood run cold. If that bastard hurt her...

"Now I can see why you might not want to take this disk and walk out of here. I figured if you were working with the cops, you'd jump at the chance to get your hands on the code and take it right to them. But you didn't. Good. Congratulations on passing the first test."

Ian heard nothing and assumed Sage was in as much shock as he was. It never occurred to him that Locke had been testing her. If she had taken the disk to leave, what would he have done to her? Ian's blood ran cold at the thought.

Whether she knew it or not, Sage had made a smart move threatening to walk out. They might have had the disk then, maybe even stopped the virus—if it actually was on the disk—but they wouldn't have gotten Locke. And Ian wanted Locke.

LOCKE LOOKED AT SARAH, turning on the charm.

"Hey, sweet thing, do you think you could excuse our girl for a moment, and let us have a moment, alone?"

Sarah looked at Sage inquiringly and shook her head in the negative.

"I'm in this one hundred percent. You can tell me whatever you tell Sage."

Locke tightened his grip on Sage's arm, and Sarah's eyes flared. Sage saw her flex her wrists and silently begged her not to lose it.

"You don't call the shots. I can send your lover here back to prison in a heartbeat, so I suggest you do as I'm telling you. Now."

Sarah looked less than happy about leaving her "lover" with Locke but left with no choice. She walked to the far corner of the bar. She wouldn't be able to hear them, but Sage knew she would keep them in eyesight.

Sage met Locke's eyes. "Why did you do that?"

Locke shrugged. "I wanted you to myself for a moment. I don't mind sharing you temporarily, but you know this thing you've got going on—" he nodded in Sarah's direction "—will have to stop."

"I love her. I don't want it to stop."

His smile was slick. "Love? Please. You're just experimenting. And besides, will she be able to provide for you, to take care of you? How else do you think you are going to get along without me? I can give you the life you've always dreamed of, baby girl. But it's just going to be you and me. Get any other ideas out of your head now."

Sage made herself appear doubtful, looking back at Sarah and then down at the table, fiddling with the colorful stick in her glass. The clinking sounds of the ice hitting the edge of the glass made her spine tingle.

"And how exactly are you supposed to do that? How do I know you won't just leave me to rot away in prison while you take off somewhere?"

Locke regarded her closely. "That won't happen." He rose, stepping before her and pulling her up to her feet in front of him, framing her face with his wiry, cold hands. Sage felt her stomach turn and she wanted nothing more than to rip herself from his grasp and run, but she held his gaze.

"I want you, baby girl. In my life. We can do great things together, have whatever we want, go wherever we want. Between us, with our talents, with the things I can teach you, we can rule the world. But you have to trust me."

He lowered his mouth to hers, and Sage sucked in a breath. She'd hoped that things wouldn't get this close, especially with Sarah acting as buffer, but as Locke insinuated his tongue between her lips, she expelled the breath and sank against him, knowing she had to.

Kissing him back was the hardest thing she'd ever had to do in her life, the price of all of her sins coming back to haunt her. But when he pulled back from her, she could tell by his rapid breathing that he'd been satisfied with her response. He spoke quietly by her ear.

"I want you to meet me later tonight. You can bring your girlfriend if you want, but we're dumping her before we leave the country."

Sage hesitated, then raised her eyes to his, wide as saucers, and nodded faintly.

"When?"

"Two o'clock at the waterfront. I'll have a boat ready down at the end of the dock, near the tour boats. We'll set fire to the Internet, baby, and then we'll leave before anyone can know."

"But my release tomorrow…"

"*I'm* releasing you. You don't need to worry about those things anymore."

She nodded. "I'll be there."

IAN WAS DYING A THOUSAND deaths, each of them painful and violent. How could he have sent them in there? What was that asshole doing to her? Not being able to hear or see after Sarah was sent away was driving him mad. How could she have agreed to leave Sage? They would talk about that.

He wanted to go there and slam through the door, and if EJ hadn't restrained him, he might have.

"They're doing okay, Ian. Back off. We can't get him if we blow it now."

Ian's chest was tight with tension. God, he was going to take that asshole down, and hard.

They got back in the car and drove a little farther down the street and saw Sage and Sarah emerge a few minutes later. The women went straight to their car and drove off. Ian wanted to follow but knew he couldn't. Locke might track them, and it had to look as though they were going back to EJ's on their own, convincing him they had sneaked out. Ian forced himself to drive away in the opposite direction, willing the time to pass quickly until he could see Sage again.

11

"WHAT DID HE WANT? Why did he send Sarah away? *Why did you leave her?*" Ian was pacing the driveway when the women drove in an hour and a half later. He was in Sarah's face the second she got out of the car, and she just stared at him incredulously. He was raving like a madman, he knew, and he didn't care. Sarah was obviously far from intimidated and ready to do battle as Ian continued his rant.

"Tell me what happened there. Now."

EJ quickly stepped between them. "Okay, hold on there, bubba, let's all go inside." EJ tried to nudge Ian in the direction of the porch, but Ian shook him off, not budging. EJ didn't move either, showing a hard edge that he rarely revealed.

"You're being an asshole, Ian. They've had a lot tougher night than you have—Sage looks like she's going to fall over. We're going inside, and you can stay out here if you want."

Ian's held his friend's cold glare and finally reluctantly agreed. Past EJ's shoulder he could see that Sage looked pale, and even in the darkness he could make out large shadows under her eyes. Her arms were wrapped tightly around herself, and she didn't meet his gaze. *Shit.*

"Okay. All right." He moved to the side. Sarah glared at him as they filed past and up to the house, and he glared back at her. As far as he was concerned, she wasn't completely off the hook yet.

"IT SOUNDS LIKE HE HAS some other plan or something is going on that he hasn't told me, won't tell me. But he's very intent on getting me on board that boat, and taking me away with him. He kept saying he could take care of me, that we could have anything we need—like he might have some significant cash stored somewhere."

Sage filled in the details of the conversations Ian and EJ had been monitoring, including the conversation after Sarah had been asked to leave. She left out Locke's kiss. She didn't even want to think about that, and besides, it wasn't relevant.

"It would be interesting to know how he plans to get that much money. Maybe he's expecting some kind of payoff for the corporate raiding he was supposedly involved in," Sarah interjected and EJ nodded.

"If we could nab him on that, he might be going away for longer than we intended, which would be sweet."

Ian listened, his mind racing as he fought the distraction of watching Sage, who was clearly exhausted. He wanted to hold her, to take back the decision to send her into that bar. And he was going to have to do it again. Shoving his fears down, he spoke, his voice cool.

"So he expects you tonight?"

"At the waterfront. He has a boat there."

"You think he'll launch the virus from the boat?"

"He wants me to launch it. That's his insurance. With my freedom in his hands, he has all the power."

"Well, then, that's what you're going to do."

Sage stared at him in amazement. "What? Are you crazy? The virus will probably bring down major—"

"I should have said that's what you'll let him *think* you intend to do—you'll have to stall him. We'll get there before anything actually happens. We just need to get him to the point of making you do it, then we have him ten ways to Sunday. We'll have access to the computer, we'll have access to Locke and we'll have him red-handed in the act. We'll set up surveillance and grab him then. If you can get him to tell you about the money—if there is any—all the better."

"Okay," Sage said, sounding weary and resigned.

"I'm going. He'll think it's weird if I don't show." Sarah spoke resolutely.

Sage shook her head. "I can say we had a fight, I'll say I snuck out on you. He wants me for himself—he said we were going to get rid of you. He might hurt you."

"I'd like to see him try, the weasel. He could hurt you, too. There's safety in numbers."

Ian broke into the conversation. "No one's getting hurt. EJ and I will be there, and this time we'll have police backup and the Coast Guard at the ready. Sarah's right, it's safer if it's two on one."

Sarah sat back, smug, but her smugness was erased when Ian turned to her, his voice brooking no argument.

"Just don't go cowboying it—you ride according to the rules and you don't leave each other, period. And don't get sidetracked."

Sarah's cheeks burned with embarrassment. "Hey, that thing with the guys at the bar—"

Ian cut her off. "If you want to be part of this team, you're going to have to learn to take orders. From me. You can't go off half-cocked, getting in people's faces and drawing unnecessary attention. You need to stay on message, Sarah."

Sarah dropped back in her chair, glaring but biting her lip self-consciously and nodding. Ian felt a little sting of conscience at coming down on her so hard in front of the others, but he was concerned about her ability to perform if she was going to run around with a chip on her shoulder. For her safety and Sage's, he had to make it clear to her what her part in this was.

The awkwardness around the table was thick, until Sage rose, her chair scraping across the floor, startling all of them. Her voice was low, lacking any intonation. She didn't look at him.

"We only have a few more hours then. I need to rest up."

Ian's gaze followed Sage until she disappeared through the doors.

Sarah's voice was soft. "I'm sorry, Ian. You're right.

I let my temper get the best of me and I shouldn't have. I'll stick by Sage tonight. We're going to get this guy."

Ian knew she would. "Why don't you guys go get some rest, as well," he said wearily. "This is going to be a late one."

"What about you?"

"I have some calls to make. See you at oh-one hundred. Set your alarms." He took out his cell phone, dismissing them effectively, and they rose to leave without a word.

"Wait," he called out as they reached the door. Sarah stopped and he asked the question that was driving him crazy. "I have to know. Did he…touch her?"

Sarah paused and quietly nodded, then walked out of the kitchen. Within moments he was alone, his voice low and determined as he made arrangements for what would go down later that night.

SINCE SHE'D GONE UPSTAIRS Sage had been standing in her room in front of the closed window. She had no intention of sleeping, as if she could. As she stared out into the darkness, she wondered—was Locke out there even now, spying on her? Her skin crawled thinking of it.

The memory of Locke's cold, possessive touch, played over and over in her mind. Needing to rid herself of the feel of his hands crawling over her body, she went into the bathroom and stepped into the shower, turning on a full blast of hot water. As she scrubbed her skin raw, she sobbed, gulping for breath. She'd made such a mess of her life, sometimes it felt as if it would only get worse.

She jumped, panicked, as she sensed another presence. Ian was there, his tortured gaze fixed on her. *I need you,* she thought and didn't even try to disguise it.

As they stared at each other, he didn't bother taking his clothes off but came into the shower, pulling her close and holding her tightly. She collapsed against him, finally giving in to his gentleness and her need to lean on someone. Regardless of anything that had been said between them, regardless of the past or the future, she knew she could lean on Ian.

And she did, letting the last tears drain from her as he just held her tightly until she could breathe again and the water began to turn cold. He didn't let go of her as he reached behind himself with one hand and shut the spray off. His voice was rough with regret.

"I'm so sorry I got you into this."

She attempted a half smile. "Actually I think I was the one who got me into this. Remember it was my idea to help trap Locke." The massive solidness of him was so comforting. She never wanted to move from this spot. "I'm okay, Ian. It was just rough…seeing him again. But I'm good. I'm ready."

Admiration washed through him at her bravery and toughness. "You're free, you know, Sage. No matter what happens tonight, no matter what happens tomorrow, there's no way I'll let anything take your freedom away from you again. I know it never should have been taken in the first place. You deserve to be free."

Sage couldn't believe her ears. She knew Ian had heard Locke admit to setting her up, yes, that's what she'd wanted. But she'd never expected him to say the things he was saying to her now. Never dared to hope. She swallowed, her response seeming silly and small to her ears.

"Thank you."

He lowered his lips to her cheek, planting a soft kiss but also licking away a drop of moisture, hearing her catch her breath at the contact. He nuzzled her, still not letting her move even a hair's width away from him. His chest rose and fell in a deep sigh.

"He put his hands on you. I'm sorry for that, too."

She shook her head vehemently. "I don't want to think about that." She raised her face to his. "I want you to touch me, Ian. Make love to me, please. I want *your* hands on me."

He gathered her impossibly closer, burying his face in her neck, and she lifted, wrapping her legs around him. Her voice was urgent, pleading.

"Wipe his touch away, Ian. Take it all away. I only want you. You make me feel free."

Twisting around in the small space of the shower, he groaned deeply, pressing her back up against the tile, and found her mouth in a savage kiss. Sage met him on equal ground, burning for his touch, desperate to forget anything and everything else but this man who held her and made her feel things she never expected to feel. *Needed. Cared for.*

She didn't dare let her mind trip over the next thought, though her heart was unafraid and whispered it to her anyway.

He is everything. To her. Somewhere in the midst of all the game playing, deception and fear, she had fallen in love with Ian Chandler.

The realization should have scared her. She had no indication that he loved her or felt anything more than he ever had. She could be setting herself up for a world of hurt. But instead her heart sang, and she felt more alive than she ever had in her life. She laughed against his lips, rejoicing, devouring him, opening herself and letting him know that she was his completely.

Ian didn't know what had changed between them, but it was consuming him. He couldn't get close enough, plundering her soft mouth, taking everything she was giving him. She moved hungrily, holding on to him as if her life depended on the contact.

He realized that while he'd taken her before, this was the first time she was really giving herself to him. The knowledge softened the edge of his desire, burning as it was. Swinging her around, he carried her back into the bedroom.

Sage didn't say anything as he laid her back on the bed, stepping back to strip off his own soaked clothing. Reaching into the pocket of his slacks, he grabbed a condom he'd picked up in EJ's bathroom on his way upstairs. He set it on the table next to the vases of fresh flowers placed in the room earlier in the day.

Naked, Ian stood before the bed, drinking in the sight of Sage.

She met his gaze directly, never breaking the visual contact as she stretched like a cat over the soft cotton sheets. She ran a hand over her smooth stomach, then lower, grazing the shadowy triangle of hair.

Like a man in a trance he followed her hand as it moved over her skin. Reaching out, her hand lifted, her fingers weaving with his as she tugged him down gently, smiling. He'd never seen her look more beautiful and he knew this time it was going to be different between them. He didn't think about why but just lost himself in the magic of her spell.

He bent over her, almost too excited to know where to start, wanting to touch her everywhere. He touched his mouth to the firm skin of her stomach, kissed her reverently there, tracing a path up to her breasts, where he closed his lips over the sweet, hot bud of her nipple and sucked until she arched up under him. Sliding one arm underneath her, he supported her while he laved and suckled her tender flesh.

When he nipped her lightly, she moaned, quivering in his arms. He smiled, setting out on a journey over every inch of her body, touching everywhere, tasting all the sweetness she had to offer, until she was writhing beneath him.

Reaching over to grab the packet, he sheathed himself quickly, and levering himself up over her, he

nudged her thighs apart with his knee and lay between
them, looking deeply into her face, framing her features
with his hands as he nudged his heat against hers.

"Open your eyes, Sage. Look at me."

She did, and he felt some part of himself open, con-
necting with her on a deeper level than he had ever
connected with anyone, any woman, before. She looked
at him with such absolute trust in her eyes, such open
desire, that he felt the weight of it in his soul. He lowered his lips to hers, falling into her gaze as his mouth
caressed hers and he eased his hard length inside her.

Slowly, gently, he deepened the kiss as he sank into
her. She moved against him slightly, clenching him and
sighing. The pleasure was exquisite, but something
even more profound than that made him determined to
extend this experience as long as he possibly could.

Sage was in heaven. Encompassed by Ian's warmth,
feeling the solid maleness of him inside and out, he became her world and she never wanted to leave this spot.
Love and passion mixed headily as she rotated her hips
against his, urging him to move with her. Shimmering
sparks of pleasure shot through her with every slight
movement, her entire body responding in unison to his.

His eyes were like molten silver, fixed on hers as he
thrust deeper. She wrapped her legs around his waist,
hitching herself up higher, planting her hands back
against the thick headboard to provide maximum resist-
ance against his long, confident thrusts.

She felt the tight tension in her body suddenly burst
as she came, the strong waves of orgasm pulsing

through her limbs. Needing to be closer, she clutched his shoulders.

His skin was gleaming with perspiration, every muscle in his body defined as he held himself tense above her, maintaining control over his own pleasure for the sake of hers. She beckoned him to come back down to her.

"Kiss me, Ian. Hold me. I want to feel you come inside me."

His eyes flared at her words as he descended, his mouth consuming hers as he thrust harder. He was so deep inside of her, filling her, giving himself over to her so passionately that she cried out, helpless against the pleasure winding its way through her body again.

His mouth was by her ear, and he was breathing heavily, barely able to form words, but he did, urging her along with him.

"Come…come with me, come, Sage…say my name, *say it….*"

She said it over and over, letting his loving erase anything else that had touched her mind or body, letting herself be claimed by him, and claiming him in return. Nothing existed except Ian.

He licked her earlobe, chanting into her ear as he kissed her in that overly sensitive spot, his words mirroring his hard thrusts that pushed her over the brink just as his chant turned into a long growl of release. His arms were around her like steel bands as they rocked together. She burrowed against him, not wanting to let go.

"Oh…my…God…" His voice was still ragged with pleasure as he continued to move inside of her as if he could never stop. She squeezed him, hugging him with her whole body, sighing as little remnants of pleasure continued working their way over her skin and love blossomed in her heart, full and unafraid of anything, including the future.

He stopped moving and started to lift off her, but she held him firmly there.

"No, don't move."

"I'm too heavy."

She shook her head, wondering if he was remembering how she had pulled away from him before, how she had said she didn't like the closeness afterward. Those fears seemed foreign to her now.

"You're not. I like it."

He tentatively relaxed against her, kissing her face, searching for the least bit of discomfort he could be causing her. But she just kissed him back and nestled against him. Finally he did relax, though he shifted much of his weight to her right side, and she fell asleep in the warm burrow of his body.

Ian, however, did not sleep. He studied the peaceful features of the woman he held. They had only a few hours left together. Touching her face lightly, he knew he wasn't going to put her through one more moment of hell if he could spare her that. God knew, he'd caused her enough.

He felt his heart seize remembering what she'd had to do and how she'd been weeping in the shower. It wasn't going to happen again. He stayed awake for a while, thinking and planning, until finally disengaging himself from her embrace, picking his still wet clothes up from the floor and going to get ready.

SAGE MUMBLED INTO THE pillow when the pounding sound wouldn't go away. Jeez, would someone make that stop?

Then it got worse—the pounding became a shaking—and her eyes flew open. She gasped when she saw someone standing before her.

"Sage, it's just me, Sarah. Calm down. Here."

Sage pulled on the robe that Sarah was handing her. Oh, God—it must be time. The realization startled her awake.

"I'm sorry...I forgot to set the alarm...." Still groggy but realizing what was at stake, she stood up too fast and wove slightly before sitting back down on the edge of the bed. "Shit."

"You sleep like the dead, woman. I thought I was going to have to dump something over you. But you have to snap to, it's urgent. EJ's getting ready. We have to go."

Sage prodded her brain to work. "Let me get dressed. Where's Ian?"

Sarah snorted and threw her a shirt from the dresser. "That's the million-dollar question."

Sage was awake now. "What do you mean?"

"I wasn't sleeping—I felt, you know, kinda cruddy about that stuff that happened earlier—and about fifteen minutes ago I heard a door close and footsteps and saw Ian heading out the door. He took off on foot. Alone."

Sage wrinkled her brow. Fifteen minutes? She looked at the clock and groaned. That's why she was so dead asleep—she'd only passed out in Ian's arms less than an hour ago. A tingle worked its way over her skin as she remembered what they'd shared, and she shook her head, trying to make sense of what Sarah was saying.

"Maybe he was just going to the station for something he forgot? I'm not supposed to meet Locke for an hour yet."

Sarah shook her head. "Why wouldn't he drive then? He looked like a man on a mission—all geared up so I barely saw him, head to toe in night gear. I think he's gone on without us. He was heading toward the waterfront."

"He's going to take on Locke alone."

"That sounds about right." EJ's voice interrupted them from the doorway. He was also decked out, as Sarah called, in "night gear," and suddenly Sage felt a little obvious in the bright blue tank Sarah had tossed at her.

"What are we going to do?"

EJ blew out a breath, his face tense. "If Ian has gone ahead, he's probably going to try to sneak in and lay in wait for Locke. Or take him early by surprise."

Sage paced the room.

"We have to go help him."

"That's a little hard to do when we don't know what

his plan is," Sarah huffed, crossing her arms in front of her indignantly. "So who's the one going off half-cocked now? That guy has some nerve."

EJ shook his head. "Ian's experienced. He knows what he's doing, but he still should have clued us in. I have a feeling his emotions might be clouding the issue more than he thinks." He looked at Sage meaningfully, and she just turned away to brush her hair quickly.

"Should we call Marty?"

EJ was quiet as he apparently considered their situation. As the only one in the room with any law-enforcement experience—even though it was years ago—he was the logical choice to be the stand-in team leader.

"No, if they try to scramble and send troops in early, it could tip Locke off. Better to stick to the original plan, especially since we have no idea what Ian's up to yet."

"So we're the cavalry?" Sarah arched an eyebrow, trying to look cool, but her obvious excitement at the prospect infused her question.

"Looks like."

"What's the plan?"

"We'll go down to the waterfront. Once we're there, we can either intercept him or at least keep an eye on what's happening and do what we need to from that point. We have to get a grasp on the situation before we make any other decisions. I have some radios we can bring in case we get separated."

Sage suddenly felt a clog form in her throat. It was hard to breathe. Noting her distress, EJ came to her side, quietly talking her out of the anxiety attack that engulfed her as she thought about Ian confronting Locke alone. What if Locke hurt him? What if the unimaginable happened?

"He's going to be fine, Sage. He's done this a hundred times with much more dangerous perps."

Sage nodded mutely and pulled herself together. "I know. Let's go. I'm ready."

She followed EJ out of the room. Sarah was already halfway down the stairs, eager to get on the road. Sage took a deep breath, steadying her nerves. She had been nervous enough when she'd thought they had a plan and now she didn't know what to expect. Before they left, EJ disappeared into the study, motioning to her to wait. Moments later he appeared back through the door.

"Change your mind about that phone call?"

He shook his head and patted his hip. "No. Bringing along another sort of reinforcement."

When she realized he meant a gun, she shivered. "Do you really think that's necessary?"

"Better to be safe than sorry."

Sage walked out of the room behind him, feeling about as unsafe as she ever had.

12

CRUNCHED BEHIND a Dumpster at the edge of the park, Ian lay on the damp grass, looking down over the dock. The river glimmered under the moon, and mosquitoes buzzed around his head, but he barely noticed, his attention on the sailboat at the end of the dock. He wondered how Locke had gotten his hands on such a beauty—probably he'd stolen it. Or bought it with stolen money. Either way, it would be more evidence against him.

There were only a few boats latched to the moorings, and this one stuck out like a sore thumb—the only recreation boat among the fishing vessels. Locke really was arrogant—he didn't think anyone would be looking for him or he didn't care. The boat was also the only one with a light on in the middle of the night. A cool blue light that looked like a computer screen glowing in a dark room.

Ian's gut told him he'd found the right boat. For the last half hour there'd been no movement at all. Locke was either sleeping or he wasn't on the boat.

Or it was a trap.

Even if that was the case, Ian planned on walking into it—he was ending this tonight.

When this situation was resolved, he was going to be not only speaking forcefully in Sage's defense but also hopefully providing enough evidence against Locke and how he'd set her up to take the fall to bolster his request to have her criminal record either dropped or at least sealed from the public view. She was going to have her shot at a successful life; he'd see she wasn't heading out into the world with a felony conviction weighing her down. She'd be free. Free of the past, free of Locke. And free of him.

The thought caused a little twist in his gut, but he knew it was the right thing to do. She'd wasted enough of her life. Now was time for her to go out and live it.

But first he had to get to that computer, disable the virus—if he could—or force Locke to do it. He double-checked the pistol he'd attached firmly to his side. He wasn't taking any chances—this guy was going down, tonight. Raising himself stealthily from the ground, he ambled forward, heading toward the boat.

He didn't get far when something tugged at his ankle and he did a swift spin, falling to the ground and pulling his gun. Luckily there was enough light for him to recognize EJ's pissed-off expression.

"What, you take off to cowboy this deal on your own and now you're going to shoot me?"

Ian glowered and put his gun back in the holster.

"What the hell are you doing here? You could blow

this whole thing with a stunt like that. Or get yourself shot."

"You're not trigger-happy—I was pretty sure you'd check to see who I was first."

"Glad you have faith in me. Now why the hell are you here? And where are Sage and Sarah?"

EJ thumbed back to the parking lot. "In the truck. Waiting on my signal." He gestured to the radio attached to his jacket pocket. "Sarah saw you take off from the house. Not quite as stealthy as you think in your old age," he said, answering Ian's unspoken question.

"Well, you can just go back there with them."

EJ peered to the end of the dock toward the sailboat. "Looks like Locke isn't bothering to hide all that well. It's probably a trap."

Ian rose and then turned, hissing. "Listen, I'm doing this alone. Stay out here and make sure Sage is okay."

"Don't be an idiot, Ian. You know it's stupid to go in there alone. We're supposed to be a team, right? Or is this how you always plan for it to work? You leave us behind and head out on your own?"

The comment hit home, but Ian shook it off.

"This is different. I'm not putting Sage on the line again. I shouldn't have done it earlier. I can handle Locke myself."

"She's tough. And she's worried about you."

"All the more reason for her not to be here. She could get hurt, EJ. Go make sure she's safe. Please. You shouldn't have left them back there alone—we don't know where Locke is or what he has planned."

"Okay. But here—" EJ tossed Ian the radio and looked away, giving in reluctantly "—we're thirty seconds that way. If you need us, just hit the button."

"Will do."

SAGE AND SARAH SAT ON pins and needles, waiting for some sound to emit from the small radio that Sarah had a death grip on, but it remained silent. Sage sighed impatiently.

"We should go. They might need us."

"You're right, let's—"

The door to the truck opened as she reached for the handle, and Sage nearly jumped out of her skin. It was EJ.

"You found him?"

EJ nodded. "He wants to hit the boat alone. He has the radio, he'll call for backup if he needs it."

"How could you let him go in there alone? What if we can't get there in time?" Sage's anxiety levels were busting through the roof, and it was reflected in her voice. EJ put a calming hand on her shoulder.

"He knows what he's doing. This could work. The boat looked unoccupied, and if Ian can get in there and assess the situation, this could go easier than we expected."

"Or it could be a trap."

EJ raised an eyebrow at Sage's acuity for understanding the situation. "Could be. But Ian knows that and he'll react accordingly. It's only a trap if you don't suspect it."

"Hmm. Oh…" She put a hand to her stomach, pressing lightly.

"What?"

Sage looked down, seeming embarrassed. "I, uh, have to go."

"Now? Here?"

She shrugged. "You guys rousted me out of bed so fast that I didn't have a chance. And I think all this is getting to my stomach—I don't feel too well."

EJ eyed her speculatively. "Nice try, but we're all staying here."

Sage pressed the case, glaring at him. "I am going to the bathroom. There's one over there, in the marina. It's lit and you can see me. You can go with me if you want, I don't care, but I'm *going*."

"Fine, I will go along. I'll take a pit stop as well."

"Okay, I'm not staying here by myself," Sarah piped in.

Moments later they were walking quickly across the wet grass toward the small white building where the restrooms were housed. Sage wished she'd seen EJ return so she would know for sure which direction he'd headed back from. But she had seem him leave, so she had some idea where to go. However, for the moment she played it cool and stopped by the edge of the building, making her case appear urgent. She hoped to hell there was a window, and if not, she'd have to work something out while they took their turns. "Me first."

EJ nodded, and Sarah looked around, peering into the darkness that surrounded them. Sage disappeared into the small building.

Inside she saw there was a slim window above the toilet—luck was with her. It would be a tight fit, but she could make it. She flushed the toilet to mask any noise she might make and quickly ambled up and over the sill. She rolled out and hit the ground with a thud, sharp edges of brush scraping her skin, but she barely felt it. Then she was around the corner of the building, running for her life—or maybe for Ian's. She had to help—Locke wanted her and he would stop at nothing to have her.

Looking back, she saw EJ pulling at the locked door, knocking. She didn't have long before they figured it out. Running, she soon found the sailboat at the end of the dock—and the dark figure moving past the window on the other side of the curtain. Was it Ian? Or Locke?

IAN WAS TOO LATE. He stared at the screen, the lines of code spinning before him—the virus had been executed. Locke had set it off early. He cursed, then looked closer. On another laptop on a separate table, it wasn't computer codes but numbers—bank transactions—that were flashing on the screen.

He sat, hitting a few keys, and watched as the sums in the accounts grew larger by pennies, then by dollars. A few more keystrokes and he felt the sinking in his chest—all the bank accounts were in Sage's name. Offshore, illegal bank accounts. For a moment his head spun with the new information, then a red-hot anger settled in his gut.

Locke was doing it again—using her to set up his own scam. The virus wasn't going to disable electronic purchases or send any kind of social message, it was simply bilking hundreds of thousands of dollars—and probably millions by the time it was done—a few pennies at a time from accounts all over the world.

This is how Locke planned on supporting himself and Sage—and getting her to stay with him for as long as he wanted. He could potentially hold this over her head forever.

"I see you've discovered my surprise. It really was a gift for LadyBug, but you haven't spoiled it. I always have a contingency plan."

Ian turned slowly, his hand at his waist, and he heard the telling click of a gun being cocked. Locke was standing directly in front of him—he hadn't heard him approach. He must have been waiting, watching, hiding in the boat's closet. *Shit.*

"You can just slide that over to me, on the floor. Slowly."

"It won't hold up. You can't do it to her again, Locke. You played your card getting her to take the fall for you once. It won't happen again."

Locke laughed. "You're wrong. I could manage to send her away for a very long time—ruin her life completely. But that's not what I want. I love her, you know, and I just managed to find a way to keep her with me and live in style."

"She'll never go with you, and I'll never let her take the rap for this."

Locke clucked condescendingly. "Oh, you haven't gone and fallen in love now, have you? What a pity, seeing as I'll probably have to kill you. That will be hard on LadyBug. She has a soft heart, I think, in spite of how she comes across. But don't worry—I'm more than man enough to make her forget you."

Ian's anger flashed, but he choked it down. He had to find a way to stall, to signal the others with the radio clipped to his jacket. Trying to appear unconcerned, he laughed.

"Love? Hardly. But she was sweet, I'll give you that. But you'll never get your hands on her—she's not coming."

He could hear Locke suck in an angry breath, spitting out one word. "What?"

"I'm solo on this one, you jerk-off. It's just you and me. I changed the plan. Sage is under watch by another member of my team. She won't be coming out to play. She's on our side now."

"You'd better—"

Just as Ian thought to make his move, knowing he'd rattled Locke, he turned, hearing the sliding of the door opening, and his heart thundered in his ears as his instincts told him what his eyesight confirmed a second later—Sage. Somehow she'd managed to slip away from EJ and Sarah. She looked pale, but her eyes were burning brightly as she looked at him in total…*contempt?* She went to Locke's side, smiling.

"Darling. What have we here?"

Locke's eyebrow cocked, and he looked over at Sage, keeping the gun trained on Ian. "Well, well. Your friend the cop said you weren't coming. In fact, he said you were playing on his team now. Is that true?"

"He tried to keep me away, but he couldn't. There was no way I was not showing up tonight."

Ian felt a surge of revulsion as Sage slid her palm over Locke's chest.

"The tables have turned, Ian. You've screwed me, and now I'm screwing you right back." She wandered over to the computers, assessing the symbols dancing across the screen, and her eyes became wide in delight. "These are ours?"

"Yours, my sweet. A gift."

Ian broke in. "A gift? You'll go to prison for a long time for stealing that much cash, Sage. He's setting you up again."

Sage leveled a playfully dangerous look at Locke. "Would you do that to me?"

He laughed. "Yes, but as it turns out, I'll need you to access that money—it's all in your name after all. I may have written the virus and executed the plan, but the payload is all in your name, baby girl. You are a rich woman now. We can be together, do anything you want. Anywhere."

Looking like a kid on Christmas morning, Sage went over to Locke. Raising up on tiptoe, she dragged her tongue along the skin of his neck, and Ian felt his blood run cold when Locke closed his eyes and shuddered in response. And that split second she'd given Ian—and he had to believe she'd done that—was all he needed to flick the switch on the radio. Now EJ and Sarah should be able to hear them and know what was happening.

"You know, I might be able to be convinced to let this all just go away." Ian tilted his head toward the computers. "There's a lot of cash there—maybe you could see your way through to sharing some of it."

"Why would I bother?" Locke wrapped his free arm around Sage, who was still staring up at him adoringly. He then smiled at Ian, satisfaction in his eyes. Locke was high on control, believing he'd won, and that made him stupid, Ian hoped.

"Because then you two can take off without a murder rap hanging over your heads. I can disappear, and the entire thing just gets forgotten. Killing me will make it hard for you to keep a low profile."

"He's right, Locke. We could just—"

"No. I make the decisions, I make the rules."

Sage pushed away from Locke. "I never signed on for murder."

Locke pulled her back roughly, "You'll just do as you're told, baby girl. We will have enough money there to do whatever we want. The cop is just trying to save his own skin. And if you don't like that, maybe you should join him. I can always change the names on those accounts easily enough and find another body for my bed."

Suddenly Sage appeared completely outraged. Ian

hoped she knew what she was doing. "I thought I was more than that to you! I'm just another body for your bed?"

Locke shrugged. "You want to be more than that, you have to earn it."

"Anything. How?"

Locke smiled viciously. "Get the cop's gun."

Ian saw Sage swallow as her eyes searched the floor and she found the weapon and picked it up.

"Point it at him."

He watched her eyes change slightly, darkening, her pulse slamming so hard he could see it from where he stood. His gut clenched as Locke trained his pistol on Sage now.

"Shoot him."

"What?"

"Prove your loyalty to me. Shoot him."

"I d-don't know h-how." Her voice shook, and Ian looked at her panicked eyes, fearing she was going to lose it. Ian's voice was like a whip as he saw Locke's finger pressed the trigger on his own gun.

"If you shoot her, I'll kill you—you can't get both of us." Ian spoke urgently, trying to keep his voice level.

Locke's glanced toward him was contemptuous. "I guess we'll just have to see. *Shoot him,* Sage."

Sage stared into Ian's eyes, her pupils dilated fully, her face drained of any color as she pulled the cylinder back, her movements robotic. She was breathing more heavily now, and Ian just hoped if she got a shot off she could miss him or not wound him mortally, though the quarters they were in were pretty cramped. If she pulled it off, she'd have to move fast enough to avoid Locke's shot.

Seconds later, chaos ensued. Ian heard something smash and realized Sage had squeezed the trigger and shot the laptop on the table behind him. Since the screens provided their only light, the room became that much darker, and almost within the same second Ian launched himself forward toward Locke, slamming into him just in time to hear another shot fired. His heart stopped as he looked around wildly, searching for Sage, the acrid odour of gunshot everywhere.

He couldn't see her and he yelled her name like a madman, trying to see where she'd fallen. *Please let her be all right*. The words became a chant as he searched the room. Before he could make out what was happening, he felt a solid slam to his head and he pitched backward into the dark, banging into the table. More noise—he looked up to see EJ and Sarah crashing down the stairs of the cabin. But what had hit him?

Blinking to clear his vision, he saw EJ, gun drawn, standing next to Sarah, staring toward the other end of the cabin. Ian followed his glance and felt his heart plunge. Someone had hit a light switch and the small room was brightly lit again—enough so that Ian could see why EJ and Sarah were staring with such horror.

Sage had been hit.

Ian trained his mind not to panic and assessed the wound from a distance. It was a shoulder entry, not fatal, but she had passed out. Locke knelt by her, pulling her up next to him, his gun pressed against her temple.

"Drop your gun, hero," he instructed EJ. EJ's eyes met Ian's and Ian nodded. EJ's gun clattered to the floor. Locke moved forward, dragging Sage's dead-weight with him.

"You so much as move, she's dead. Get out of my way. Now!"

Ian saw Locke was on the edge—he had murder in his eyes—and motioned EJ and Sarah to move away from the door. Locke headed to the door.

"Leave her here. We won't follow," Ian said.

Locke laughed, and blood dribbled from his lip where Ian must have knocked him over. He was covered with other blood, as well—Sage's blood. "You're right. She's my insurance of that."

"No, just the opposite. You take her, I won't stop coming after you. I won't stop until you're dead." Ian pinned Locke with his gaze. "Locke, if you love her, let us help her."

"Please, save it. She'll be lucky if I don't drop her overboard for the sharks. But you'll just have to take your chances on that, won't you?"

Locke pulled Sage's unconscious form roughly up the stairs and exited the boat. The three of them followed quickly, but he already had Sage in a small motorboat on the other side of the dock and was pulling off, out into the blackness of the river.

Ian could see Sage sprawled across the bottom of the boat, and there was no way he was letting her disappear.

He turned on EJ and Sarah, shouting, "Go! Get backup, I'm going after them."

They didn't have a chance to respond as Ian jumped down into another boat, leaning down to mess with the wires until the vessel sputtered to life and Ian disappeared into the wide river, praying he could catch up with Locke before it was too late.

SAGE AWOKE FEELING flipped around like a pancake, her body throbbing and her stomach churning each time she rolled against the side of something hard. It was so noisy, cold and dark. Prying her eyes open, she used every spare bit of energy she had—which wasn't much—to brace herself against another knock into whatever it was she kept slamming into. She was too groggy to even be disoriented.

Taking a few deep breaths, she kept the lurching of her stomach at bay, though as she did that, a screaming pain in her arm and side caused blackness to dance in front of her eyes again. Christ, where was she and what had happened?

Her eyes flew open when it all came rushing back into her mind—she'd shot at Ian or past him, as far as she knew, and then all she remembered was something burning into her, knocking her back, and then nothing. Where was she now? Where was Ian?

Peering up, she saw treetops racing by overhead. As her mind cleared, she realized she was in a boat, though it wasn't the boat she had been on before. How had she been moved? Trying to push herself up, she groaned as her arm wouldn't support her and the pain was excruciating. She looked down and saw that her skin was covered with blood, a large slash in her arm caked and raw with it. Her stomach flipped again—she'd been shot.

Locke.

Terror fought with the need to stay alert as she pulled herself up with her other arm, sitting up against the side of the motorboat speeding over the waves. She squinted, her head swimming. It had to be Locke at the wheel of the boat.

The engine had masked her movements, and Locke had no idea she was conscious, his attention on steering the boat. She sat still, wondering what to do. She could throw herself over if she had enough strength, but where was she? And could she realistically make it to shore with her arm? She could try to take him out from behind, though she doubted she could move quietly enough or even stand upright. If he lost control of the boat, they could both be killed.

She wished she could remember how she got there—it couldn't be good if she was there and shot and Locke had escaped. Ian never would have let him take her—this she knew. And her chest tightened as tears burned her eyes—what if she hadn't missed? What if she'd shot Ian by mistake? Or what if Locke had gotten the best of him? So much for her brilliant interference.

And where had EJ and Sarah been? It just didn't make sense that Locke could have gotten away with her in tow if everyone was okay. A sense of helplessness overwhelmed her. She felt so alone. Stifling a sob, she pushed her fears to the back of her mind and let the need for survival surge to the surface.

She had to find a way out of there, somehow to get away from Locke. It looked as though she was going to have to try to hoist herself overboard. Pushing herself up a little more, she tried to gauge her distance from the motor; she'd have to push herself away from the boat to remain safe from the blades. She might drown, she might attract predators who were looking for their nightly meal, but at least she wouldn't be stuck here waiting for whatever fate Locke had in store for her.

She pushed herself up to the edge and managed to crawl up over a bench, hanging on the inside of the boat and staring down at the waves. She peered cautiously at Locke and then hoisted herself up a little farther, when another noise entered the din and she was blinded by spray shooting up the side of the boat.

Sage shrieked when another boat flew up alongside of the one she was in and slammed into it, sending her flying across the middle, the resulting pain of the fall nearly knocking her unconscious again. Grabbing on to the first thing she could find—she could hardly stay steady as the boat pitched about—she looked forward. There was no driver!

She scuttled backward, barely avoiding the two large bodies that hurtled toward her. Someone had jumped into their boat from the boat that had crashed into them and was now locked in battle with Locke. Adrenaline allowed her to push herself up against the bench again, and she pitched forward, falling again but landing closer to the wheel.

"You son of a bitch, did you really think I'd let you take her?"

She looked up to see Ian's bloodied face just as he was slamming a fist into Locke's face. Locke fell backward but came up swearing, hurling himself at Ian, and nearly taking both of them over the side. Sage leaped toward the steering wheel, grabbing it in time to swerve them in the opposite direction, landing the men back in the center of the vessel.

She couldn't see everything that was going on, but she heard one more sickening crack and a dull thud. Her stomach turned and she was loath to look in case it would be Locke staring back at her.

Unsure of where she was going, she pulled back on the throttle and slowed the boat to a stop in the middle of the river before collapsing back down on the seat near the wheel.

"Sage…Sage, oh, God, are you all right?" Ian's voice was slurred and she whipped around, ignoring the sharp stab of pain in her head as she did so, tears springing to the surface freely as she saw him standing victoriously over Locke's crumpled form. He made his way carefully over to her.

"I—I don't know… You?" She didn't recognize her own voice, but before he could answer, lights blinded them and a storm of noise surrounded the boat as a helicopter came in low over them and a police boat pulled up alongside.

Then Ian was beside her, holding her up, holding her against him, and then she remembered how to breathe. The ordeal was over. She sagged against him and winced as his hand closed over her shoulder to support her.

"Oh, God, sorry, sweetheart. Here, sit, someone will be along to help soon. You're going to be okay."

She slumped down onto the seat, watching some men pull up next to the boat, and Ian went to meet them. It felt colder when he left her, and she wanted nothing more than to have him back, close by and keeping her warm.

The group of officers spoke for a few minutes, and she saw EJ and Sarah climbing off the police boat behind them, huddling around Ian and then heading in her direction. Sage opened her mouth to say something to them but felt her consciousness drift, her vision blur and her body start to go slack again. Sarah sat down and pulled her upright.

"Hey, there, sista, hold on now. You give us the slip and see what happens?" Sarah's voice was teasing but tense.

Sage fought the battle for consciousness, her mind focused on one thing and one thing only. "Where's Ian?"

"He had to take care of business, but something tells me he won't be away for long. Just hang in there."

"How did I end up here?"

EJ's voice was gentle as he sat down on her other side, helping support her. "I'm not one hundred percent sure how it happened, but when we showed up, it looked like you three were in some kind of tussle. And when the lights went on, Locke had you with a gun to your head—he used you as a hostage to escape. We couldn't do anything or he would have killed you."

Sage took a deep breath—a deep, painful breath. "I don't remember any of that. I just woke up rolling around in the bottom of the boat. I was going to jump, then Ian was here…. Very confusing…" Her voice faded again as everything blurred, and she groaned, frustrated. She wanted to know what had happened, what was going on, but her head and body were not co-operating.

She looked up—there were two Sarahs now, actually. She furrowed her brow, concentrating so she could try to form one image again, but then Sarah was gone altogether and strong hands were holding her again.

Ian's hands. Sage blinked, struggling to remain aware, and saw another man kneel down in front of her, shining a bright light in her eyes. She twisted her head away in surprise, but Ian shushed her, comforting her.

"Whoa, there, darlin', take it easy. Sage, you're hurt. Let them check you out, okay? The medics are going to take you to the hospital to get cleaned up and checked out."

She nodded, her head heavy, but she fought it. "You, too?"

"I'll be with you, don't worry. I won't leave."

Knowing that, Sage felt a whole lot better already.

13

SAGE ALWAYS THOUGHT IT was corny when people said that they felt more alive, that things tasted better, felt better and that everything was more intense after a near-death experience, but she would never scoff at those people again. Especially now that she was one of them.

Well, almost. The injuries she'd sustained going head-to-head with Locke hadn't been fatal, but she'd come close enough. It had only been eight days, and yet she felt as if it was a lifetime ago. Everything was different now. Locke was in the hands of federal authorities, for one, and she was not only alive and well, she was free as a bird.

Sitting on the stony wall by Ray's hot dog stand, she treated him to a brilliant smile when he handed her a hot dog with everything on it—her second one—in celebration of her newfound freedom.

Because she'd been in the hospital, she hadn't been able to make it to her release hearing, but Ian had taken care of it for her, and it had been a done deal for four whole days now. Maybe that was why everything tasted better, she thought with glee as she took a big bite of the hot dog.

"So you a free woman now, Sage. Though maybe more free than you want to be?"

Catching some chili from her lip, she looked at Ray quizzically. "Huh? No way. Can't be too free, Ray. And the best part is it's really a fresh start. They sealed my records after they found out that Locke was the real creator of the original virus and that I helped Ian bring him in. So I don't have to even report my arrest or jail time when I look for jobs. Though I'm not sure that's what I'm doing just yet."

Ray turned away to wait on another customer and she smiled again, just because she couldn't seem to stop. The whole world was before her, and she only had to choose what she wanted.

The thought stopped her, and she sighed, dabbing at her lips with a napkin and swinging her knee under the light sundress she wore. She'd gone shopping with Sarah and bought it because it was cheerful and sexy, covered with flowers, and it reflected how she was feeling. Though that wasn't the only reason.

She remembered her first thought when she'd seen the dress was that Ian would love it. She knew without a doubt that one of the things she wanted in her new life was him. But she wasn't sure he was on board with that plan.

She hadn't seen him at all since he'd left her at the hospital, but he'd called and checked on her and said he'd meet her there today after he finished some business.

In all fairness, he'd been gone the better part of the

week, accompanying Locke to D.C., where federal authorities had taken over, and Ian had to wrap up his job there before returning to Norfolk for good. She wondered if he would be leaving her behind with all the other things from his past or if she could persuade him to be part of her new future.

"See there, that's what I was talking about. That look you've got—you may be free, missy, but your heart belongs to that FBI man you've been flirting with all these years, huh? Did he finally turn around and catch you for good?" Ray laughed a little as he wiped down his already sparkling stand.

Sage shook her head. "I think he may just be letting me go, Ray. He wants a new start, too, to be free. I'm part of a life he's leaving behind."

"Now, now, what have I told you about thinking like that? Don't give up too easily, li'l girl. Things gonna work out just fine."

"How can you know that, Ray?"

"Because I know you. And if you love him, he'd be an idiot to let you go. And the man don't sound stupid."

Sage smiled and laughed softly. "No, he's not stupid. But we'll see, Ray. We'll see."

IAN WATCHED SAGE FROM the window of the coffee shop he'd sat at when Locke had first appeared. Watching her seemed to be a habit he couldn't quite break.

She was eating lunch with Ray, bright and cheerful in her new summer dress, and his breath caught when she laughed. She was the most beautiful woman he'd ever known, and he was dumb with love for her. He'd known it the last time they'd made love, known she was the only woman who had ever touched him so deeply, who'd become more important than anything in his life and who'd given herself to him so completely. Made him want to give himself to her in return.

And he had to let her go.

Closing her case and sealing her records had been almost easy in the face of the evidence and Locke's arrest. So now she was finally free and she could go anywhere, do anything she wanted. He wasn't about to stand in the way of that.

He closed his eyes, images of that night still fresh in his mind. When he'd pulled up alongside Locke's boat and seen her ready to fall over the edge, he'd nearly lost it. He hadn't known what to expect before he'd seen her, preparing himself for the fact that she could already be dead, and his heart had leaped when he'd spotted her, wounded as she was. To see her hanging over the dark waters had stolen years from him. He hadn't been able to deny his feelings for her in that moment. They'd flooded him. He'd known he would have given everything, anything, just to have her alive.

The thought of losing her had driven him to jump into the other boat, though that hadn't been his first intention. But he'd just acted on instinct and he was glad. It was over now. The list of Locke's indictments was so long he wouldn't see the light of day for a very long time except through steel bars. Sage would never have to worry about him again.

"Hey, Ian. You're looking solemn for a man who just busted a major criminal and is starting a brand-new career," EJ said, sitting down next to him at the table. He looked pretty ragged himself.

"You look a little rough around the edges yourself—I take it you told Millie the wedding was off?"

EJ sighed. "Yeah. We were up all night, talking. I feel better…and worse. She didn't take it well, not that I expected her to. I don't know if we can even be friends after this. My family's just as shocked. And with the news I'm leaving the company, well…it sucks, but I shouldn't have gotten myself or Millie into this in the first place."

"I know what you mean," Ian said, looking out the window.

EJ followed his gaze, and let out a low whistle. "I knew it—you've got it bad."

"Yeah."

"So what are you going to do about it?"

"Nothing."

EJ's eyes widened. "Why the hell not? It's clear she's crazy about you, too."

Ian shook his head. "No. We were just…in the middle of things. She's free now and she deserves to be able to go out there and take her shot at life."

"Aren't you a little uncomfortable making her decisions for her? She's a big girl, you know."

"It's not like that…. Aw, can we just drop this? I take it you're here because you're going to take me up on my offer?"

"I am."

"That's good news. Who's taking over for you?"

"Grace."

"You're kidding! How'd you swing that? Not that I don't think she's the perfect choice. She is—she's wanted this forever."

EJ laughed. "Well, the board has become more liberal than I realized over the years—only Jordan Davis dug in with a negative vote, but he was unable to influence the rest of the board. Even my mother approved. I was pleased but surprised."

"Gracie must be like a kid at Christmas."

"She is. She's nervous—the board did insist on a two-year probationary period before the position is permanent—but she's up to the task. She'll really make the place hum. She's got our dad's blood for the business. It was never my thing."

Hearing the bell tinkle over the door, Ian saw Sarah walk in decked out in her jeans and black leather jacket in spite of the ninety-degree temperatures. Ian smiled. She was so cool on the outside, but he knew better— she had a hot temperament and attitude to match. He had his concerns, but he was also willing to give her a chance.

"Hey, Sarah."

"Hi."

He sighed. Her tone told him she hadn't quite forgiven him for setting off on his own, leaving them behind the night he went after Locke, after he had lectured her. It didn't seem to change her view that he was the team *leader*—she was emphasizing the word *team*.

And she was right.

"Sarah, I want to offer you the third position on the team."

Her eyes flew to EJ and she smiled widely, and he nodded, confirming. Ian continued.

"But you'll have to beef up your qualifications."

"What does that mean?"

"A six-month stint in the police academy while working on the team—you'll be basically working two full-time jobs for those six months, but since you don't have any law-enforcement training, I can't take you on without it."

"I'll do it."

Ian quirked a brow, amused but not surprised at her cool enthusiasm. "Don't you want to know the details, the hours, what the police academy is about?"

Her blue eyes regarded him steadily and she asked dutifully, "Okay, so what's it about?"

"Think of it as a high-intensity boot camp. Weapons, assault training, the works. And you will be expected to be working and training with the team, as well."

"Sounds good. I'm in."

EJ burst out laughing and Ian joined in. Sarah regarded them both as if they were crazy.

"So when do we start?"

"Meet me at the station tomorrow. You'll meet who you have to meet, get the paperwork signed and we'll get going. Is it going to be a problem for you to move so quickly?"

"No problem. I'll just have my equipment shipped. Any chance the department can pay for that?"

Ian suppressed a smile. "I'll see what we can do."

His gaze drifted out the window again, and he saw Sage, still sitting on the wall, chatting to Ray, but she was looking around. For him. He'd told her he would come by as soon as he was done. Her head turned in his direction, and though he knew it was impossible, she seemed to be looking directly at him. Ian stood, speaking distractedly to his new partners. "I'll see you two tomorrow. Nine sharp."

He barely heard them voice their agreements as he walked out of the shop.

SAGE SAW IAN CROSS THE street, his gait loose and casual, but the expression on his face was intense as he approached. She found herself smoothing the skirt of her dress somewhat nervously, wishing she didn't have the large bandage covering her shoulder where her gash was stitched and healing.

She glanced away as he came closer, composing herself, and when she did glance up again, he was standing right in front of her. The emotions in his eyes nearly undid her. She took a stabilizing breath and smiled.

"Ian. I wondered if you were going to make it."

"I had to meet with EJ and Sarah. I'm sorry to have taken so long. You had a good visit with Ray?"

She looked over at Ray, who was discreetly occupying himself with reloading his supplies.

"Yeah. We had celebratory dogs. I'm pretty stuffed."

She held her hand to her stomach, the casual chit-chat raising her tension levels so that those chili dogs were not happy.

"Are you okay?" Ian's voice was warm with concern. "Are you still feeling ill?"

"No, no. I'm fine. I'm nervous is all—I've been so nervous to see you."

His brow furrowed. "Why?"

"Because…"

I love you. And you don't love me back.

She sputtered, "Because it's just awkward, you know…how everything's changed. Having everything over."

He nodded, and her heart broke a little more. Then he held out his hand. She reached out and took it, not sure what was going to happen next.

They walked down to the waterside, not saying anything. Sage liked the feel of her hand wrapped in his— out in the open, walking like lovers who had no cares in the world, no secrets to hide. He turned to her when they were alone and out of earshot of anyone else.

"You're going to be fine, Sage. I know it must be daunting now, but it will work out."

She just stared at him—he was talking to her like she was a child. He seemed uncomfortable when she didn't respond.

"Have you thought about what you'd like to do next?"

Remembering the texture of his skin under her hands, she knew exactly what she'd like to do next.

"I'm not sure yet. Some things are still…unsettled."

"Of course. I imagine you'll be spending time with your family?"

She looked over at him, tiring of the dance, the polite conversation, and leaped. She'd had enough. Enough of the games, the deceptions and the waiting. She decided on a straight-on attack. Taking a deep breath, she spoke her thoughts loudly and clearly, never breaking eye contact.

"I love you."

His eyes widened, but he didn't say anything. She took a step closer.

"Did you hear me, Ian? Did you hear what I said? I don't know what to do next because I've fallen in love with you and I know you don't love me back, but still… I hoped…."

The tension was thick between them, and finally he hauled her up close to him, his eyes moving over her face hungrily.

"You love me?"

She nodded, and before she could take her next breath his mouth was on hers, kissing her as if his life depended on it. She heard him mutter something against her lips and drew back.

"What did you just say?"

His eyes, dark with emotion, saw into the very core of her as he spoke.

"I love you, too. I probably shouldn't even say that, but I want you to know I wasn't just using you—it wasn't just sex." He smiled a sideways kind of smile that melted her heart. "Well, I guess it was at first, but you were always more to me, more than even I knew. It nearly killed me to see you hurt, and it's killing me to have to step away from this."

"Step away? From what? You just said you love me. I said I love you. Who's stepping away?"

His eyes were too serious and she didn't like the way the atmosphere had changed between them.

"I am. This isn't going to work—the time isn't right."

"What does that mean? What—"

He cut off her question, gripping her by the shoulders, his voice resolute. "You have your whole life, anything you want available to you now. You should go get it. I want you to have everything you ever wanted."

"Fine." She stared at him stubbornly. "I want you."

He shook his head, his eyes tortured but his mouth set in a determined line. He still wanted to be the one in control of everything.

"I don't want this either, Sage. I'm starting up the new team, there's a lot going on. I'm not in a place to start a new relationship."

"So you love me but you don't want to be with me? Because of your *job?*" She stared at him, incredulous, and he stiffened defensively.

"That shouldn't come as a surprise to you."

She knew he was referring to what he'd told her about his marriage, about not being there for his ex-wife. How he'd let her down by not being there for her.

Then suddenly she realized what was happening—Ian was afraid. Afraid of loving her, afraid he might lose control, afraid he might disappoint her, afraid he couldn't handle it all. And it made her love him even more to see the glaring chink in his armor. She'd started out seducing him because she thought his sexual desire would be his weakness, but it wasn't—his weakness was his heart. His fear of hurting her or anyone ever again. He loved her, but he didn't trust himself. But she did. She trusted him with her life. Literally. She had to find some way to show him that, make him believe it.

Strategizing quickly, she looked into his face as if searching for something and simply said, somewhat coolly, "Okay."

He seemed startled by her easy capitulation, then slightly suspicious, so she just leaned in, wrapping her arms around him a deep hug lest he read too much in her expression. She inhaled his scent and squeezed tighter—there was no way she was letting him get away. She had one more play left.

"I guess you're right, but this sucks, and I don't really want to talk about it anymore, so, uh, I'm going. I just need to get away for a while."

She risked sharing one more deep look, wondering if he would make a move to make her stay, but he just looked away at the water and nodded. Sage turned and walked away, her lips twitching in a naughty smile. He wasn't going to know what hit him.

14

IAN COULDN'T BELIEVE IT. He closed his office door and studied the computer screen that he seemed unable to control.

It had been a hellish day and all he wanted to do was go home. But when he'd tried to shut down his computer, a winking female eye had appeared in the center of the screen.

He'd been hacked—but how?

It had to be an inside job; no one could get past the firewall they had set up. Someone had to be in this very office to create this kind of trouble. Or perhaps it was a joke—Sarah, he'd discovered, was full of them. She and EJ had had a good time yanking his chain more than once.

He was in no mood for levity. He was tired and, truth be told, he was lonely. He ached with it. It had been two days since Sage had walked away from him in the park, but it felt much longer. He'd been hellishly busy at work, but for the first time in his life it wasn't enough. Not nearly.

He slammed the keyboard hard in frustration and

blinked when the screen rolled and a new image appeared. A video feed. He sat in his chair, his jaw dropping.

Sage stood before him, staring out from the screen, and awareness dawned.

She'd hacked him!

Smirking, he realized it had been an inside job—no doubt she'd had help from his two partners. He could swear he'd seen Sarah snicker as she'd left his office for the day.

He heard Sage's voice warble through the speakers, and even though the technology didn't do it justice, the sultry sound washed over him, making him hard. His desire for her had only multiplied since she'd gone—must be what they meant about absence making the heart grow fonder, though _fondness_ was far too gentle a term for what Ian was experiencing at the moment. He leaned over the desk, riveted by her words and image.

"Have you missed me, Ian? I've missed you." She drawled the words in the sexiest way possible. "I need you. You're in my system like a virus, one that won't go away."

He saw she was wearing the same flowered dress she'd worn that day in the park. She smiled suggestively, sending heat waves across the space in between them. The picture divided: there were eight, then sixteen images of her filling the entire screen. He hit several keys and nothing happened. She had taken over his machine, the witch. She'd taken control of it, of him. Of his heart. He couldn't deny it any longer.

"I know you want me, Ian. I know you love me. Guess what? I love you, too."

She winked and unbuttoned a single button at the top of her dress, and he sucked in his breath. Where was she? Everything was dark around her.

"I won't stop trying to convince you. I've planned an all-out attack on your system. On your life. The only way to make it stop is to find me."

She undid a few more buttons and shimmied the dress to the floor, standing before him in a lacy black bra and sheer panties. His mouth went dry.

"Where are you?" he rasped.

But she couldn't hear him, of course. He couldn't object or argue. He couldn't even shut her off.

His fingers grasped the end of the desk in frustration. He wanted her—and yes, he loved her. He had resolved to walk away, but he was weakening by the moment. It was bad enough his memories haunted him, but to have her in front of him, beckoning and teasing him…it was more than he could stand. His life was so empty without her.

She laughed as if she knew what he was thinking and undid the clasp of her bra, letting her supple breasts fall free. He licked his lips, watching her dusky nipples pucker. Her copper curls danced in the breeze—she was outside.

As the multiple images of Sage showed her silently sliding out of her panties, he frantically searched the screen for more clues and yelled jubilantly when he found one—the blinking light behind her. It was an airport tower. Just like the one he often watched while sitting on his patio.

"Come to me, Ian."

But the image on the screen spoke to no one—he was already out the office door.

DRIVING LIKE A MADMAN, Ian tore up the road toward his house. He parked and jumped out of the car, dropping his keys and swearing furiously as he bent to search the sandy ground for them. Finding them, he dashed to the house, opening the door and heading straight for the patio.

But when he opened the sliding door, she wasn't there. The dress and underwear were left on the teak deck, and he bent, picking up the slight pieces of silk, rubbing their softness between his fingers, intoxicated by the scent that rose to greet him.

Where was she? His predatory instincts kicked in and he rose, turning slowly, wondering where she'd gone. What game she was playing? A laptop screen glowed in the darkness of his living room, and he walked back in the house, heading toward it. He hadn't even noticed it on the way in, he'd been so intent on finding her on the patio.

Walking toward the screen, he stopped in his tracks. The entire room lit up. The TV and what felt like hundreds of laptop screens, though it was only two, sparked to life with images of Sage, nude and lounging on a bed.

His bed. Upstairs.

He turned in that direction, then froze when her voice commanded him to.

"Wait. If you come to me, Ian, it's for good—it's forever."

Her eyes locked on his across the screen, dark and serious. His heart thudded so hard in his chest he was surprised he could even hear at all as she continued.

"I love you, Ian. If you decide to walk up those stairs, be sure it's what you want. I want all of you, body, heart, mind and soul. Because that's what I'm prepared to give you in return."

Ian didn't have to think about it. The time without her had left him starving and empty, and he wanted to go to her. He was sure that unless he was with her forever he would never completely be full. Nothing mattered more to him than being with her, and that knowledge carried him up the stairs.

When he reached the top, there was Sage. Warm, human and in the flesh, she lay before him, her eyes bright with tears, her smile brilliant. And it all was for him. She was his.

Entering the room, he found his voice.

"I'm a fool. How the hell could I have let you walk away?"

She smiled tremulously, lifting a hand to her lips as a small cry escaped. He crossed to her, tugging at his clothes and leaving them in a careless pile in the doorway. His body was hot and ready, but his heart urged him to savor every moment, to take his time and let her know everything he was feeling.

She was in his arms almost before he hit the mattress, and he wondered how he had ever thought he could live another day without her. He wrapped his arms around her, holding her close, soaking her in.

"I love you, I love you...." He couldn't seem to stop saying it. Those three words felt too small to express the enormous feelings that were overwhelming him. Her eyes met his as she reached up to caress his cheek with the back of her fingers in the most tender gesture he'd ever experienced.

"I love you, too. I want everything with you."

He turned his mouth to kiss her palm, capturing a finger in his mouth and nipping her lightly, his gaze possessive and filled with love and hope.

"Even children?"

She nodded, pressing herself against him, one of her soft hands drifting down to encircle his erection as her breasts pressed enticingly against his side. He groaned, pushing into her grip as she whispered against his ear while stroking him, "We can get started on that right now if you want."

Something flipped inside of him, and he tipped her head up so that he was looking deeply into her eyes. "You trust me that much? Even after what I told you about my marriage?" He dipped in, kissing her lightly. "After I let you walk away?"

She pouted prettily, her eyes full of mischief. "That

was a mistake, granted." Then she smiled, staring straight into his soul. "But I trust you with my life, Ian. And I trust you with our children's lives. I know you'll never let me down. And I'll never let you down either. Ever."

His voice was hoarse when he spoke, choked with emotion, but he didn't want to hide it. "You never could. You never did. But what about your dreams? Your work, the things you've missed, the things you want?"

He was speaking against her skin, dragging his lips over her and starting to lose himself in the passion that encompassed both of them. Her skin was so soft, so fragrant, he couldn't get enough.

She was breathless, too, but answered, "I can still have all of that, right? I was wrong about my mom and my sister—they just knew what made them happy. I never knew what would make me happy—really happy—until now."

"And, darlin', this is just the beginning," he whispered, holding her gently as they fell back onto the soft bed.

SARAH GROWLED IN frustration, grabbing the warm bottle of beer that sat beside her laptop on the makeshift desk in the small apartment on East Ocean View that she'd only rented yesterday. She had AC but no refrigerator. For now, a small red cooler held a few beverages, but all the ice had melted. Creature comforts weren't all that important to her, really, especially when she was working. She stared a hole in the computer screen. She'd almost had them—*almost.*

She was too tightly wound to relax, nervous about her impending stint at the police academy and pulling all-nighters tracking down a particular ring of Internet porn distributors she'd been after for a while. She wouldn't have much free time soon enough, so she needed to throw every spare minute into this right now. She was trying to expose a large group with lots of connections; it was going to take time, she reminded herself.

And in the meantime, a hundred more rings would pop up alongside of them. They were the worst of the worst, slugs who took advantage of innocents to make money and satisfy perverse pleasures. She'd been a victim once and now she was their worst enemy—or she would be once she had the resources and training of the local police department behind her. In just six months she'd be hunting the bastards down and she would actually have the power to do something about it. She could hardly wait.

An e-mail beep distracted her from her train of thought, her dark mood lifting when she saw the e-mail was from Sage. Sarah cast a worried glance at the clock—it was the middle of the night. Why would Sage be contacting her now?

Her eyes scanned the screen quickly, looking for signs of trouble, and then she broke into a wide grin when she realized what had Sage awake in the middle of the night. Or rather, who.

To: TigerLily@npd.org
From: FreeAsABird@vpn.com
Subject: Thank you!

Sarah—
Just a quick note, Ian's asleep. I wore him out <evil grin>. All went as planned. Thanks so much for your help getting into the office. Our secret, promise. I'm so happy I could burst.
Just think, maybe your Mr. Right is at the police academy and you don't even know it yet! Things are looking up.
Big hugs and kisses. See you tomorrow—if we make it out of bed. ;)
    Sage.

Sarah dropped back in her chair, suddenly exhausted from the blast of conflicting emotions that the e-mail left her dealing with.

For so many years she'd kept herself separate, cut off, her work her only focus. Now she had to deal with all these people, with friends and the complications they caused. She just wanted to get on with her training and her job and get to work. She had no dreams of white dresses, magnolias or handsome heroes.

Not that she begrudged others such things, but her priorities were just…different. She'd devoted her time and her life to another pursuit. And it made her happy. Maybe not in the same way as Sage was talking about, but all the same.…

She closed the e-mail and returned to her work, struggling to erase Sage's words and the uncomfortable inklings of hopes and dreams that had resurfaced in response to them. She'd left those things long behind her, for good.

* * * * *

*Look for Sarah's sizzling story in
January 2006 when Book 2 of the HotWires
miniseries is released. Pick up FRICTION
(#229) by Samantha Hunter.
And don't forget to check out her Web site at
www.samanthahunter.com.*

If you loved
The Da Vinci Code,
Harlequin Blaze brings you
a continuity with just as many
twists and turns and,
of course, more unexpected
and red-hot romance.

**Get ready for The White Star continuity
coming January 2006.**

This modern-day hunt is like no other....

If you enjoyed what you just read,
then we've got an offer you can't resist!

Take 2 bestselling
love stories FREE!

Plus get a FREE surprise gift!

Clip this page and mail it to Harlequin Reader Service®

IN U.S.A.	**IN CANADA**
3010 Walden Ave.	P.O. Box 609
P.O. Box 1867	Fort Erie, Ontario
Buffalo, N.Y. 14240-1867	L2A 5X3

YES! Please send me 2 free Harlequin Temptation® novels and my free surprise gift. After receiving them, if I don't wish to receive anymore, I can return the shipping statement marked cancel. If I don't cancel, I will receive 4 brand-new novels each month, before they're available in stores. In the U.S.A., bill me at the bargain price of $3.80 plus 25¢ shipping and handling per book and applicable sales tax, if any*. In Canada, bill me at the bargain price of $4.47 plus 25¢ shipping and handling per book and applicable taxes**. That's the complete price and a savings of 10% off the cover prices—what a great deal! I understand that accepting the 2 free books and gift places me under no obligation ever to buy any books. I can always return a shipment and cancel at any time. Even if I never buy another book from Harlequin, the 2 free books and gift are mine to keep forever.

142 HDN DZ7U
342 HDN DZ7V

Name _____ (PLEASE PRINT)

Address _____ Apt.#

City _____ State/Prov. _____ Zip/Postal Code

Not valid to current Harlequin Temptation® subscribers.

Want to try two free books from another series?
Call 1-800-873-8635 or visit www.morefreebooks.com.

* Terms and prices subject to change without notice. Sales tax applicable in N.Y.
** Canadian residents will be charged applicable provincial taxes and GST.
 All orders subject to approval. Offer limited to one per household.
 ® are registered trademarks owned and used by the trademark owner or its licensee.

TEMP04R   ©2004 Harlequin Enterprises Limited

Artist-in-Residence Fellowship—
Call for applications

She always dreamed of studying art in Paris,
but as a wife and mother she has had other things
to do. Finally, Anna is taking a chance on her own.

What Happens in Paris

(STAYS IN PARIS?)

Nancy Robards Thompson

Available January 2006
TheNextNovel.com

HN26

HARLEQUIN® *Blaze*

Three of Harlequin Blaze's hottest authors brought you the **RED LETTER NIGHTS** anthology this November.

Now get ready for more as each of these authors writes her own steamy tale....

GIVE ME FEVER
by **Karen Anders**

On sale December 2005

When Tally Addison's brother goes missing, she knows who to turn to—gorgeous cop Christien Castille. Only, when she and Christien stumble into a search for hidden treasure, she discovers she's already found hers...in him.

Coming in 2006...

GOES DOWN EASY by Alison Kent;
Book #225, January 2006

GOING, GOING, GONE by Jeanie London;
Book #231, February 2006

HBRLN1205